THE MADDY SAGA

BOOK FOUR

PONYGIRL SUMMER

BY

PAUL BLADES

Cover Art by Agnes Knox
agnesknox@simonas.se
agnes.knox@gmail.com

Dark Visions Publications
darkvisionspub@gmail.com

All characters and events portrayed in this work are
fictitious

Previously published:

Vol. I   Maddy becomes a Ponygirl
Vol. II   The Training of a Ponygirl
Vol. III   Ponygirl Champion

Watch for publication of the other books in the Maddy Saga:

Vol. V.   Ponygirl Love
Vol. VI   Ponygirl Season
Vol. VII   Ponygirl Gambit
Vol. VIII   Ponygirl Pleasures
Vol. IX   Ponygirl Peril
Vol. X   Ponygirl's Choice

Other books by Paul Blades:

Klitzman's Isle
Klitzman's Empire
Klitzman's Paradise
Klitzman's Pawn Part One
Klitzman's Pawn Part Two
The Taking of Cheryl Part One
The Taking of Cheryl Part Two: Slaver's Bait
Comfort Girl No. 4
Sacrifice to the Emerald God
The Blue Cantina: Anna's Surrender
The Warlord's Concubine

CHAPTER ONE
THE BAIT

Jackie's long, chocolate legs wrapped themselves around Jake's back, pulling him deeper and deeper into her well seasoned, well trained canal. Jake was pumping away madly while the tall, almost muscular, black jezebel called out to him, her voice echoing off the well appointed, luxurious, hotel room's walls.

"Oh, fuck me, Jake! Give it to me! Yeah! Yeah! Gimme your cock, honey! Slam it in me!"

Jake was doing his obedient best. It's not that he was into being dominated by $2,000 a night strumpets, it was just that Jacqueline knew how to drive him wild.

He had come back to Chicago on a mission. It was about four months since he received a telephone call from billionaire Michael Burnham that his niece, Maddy, had been kidnapped. Jake was a fixer. He had a hard crew and a cold heart. He and his men, all hand picked for personal loyalty to him and their own sense of ruthlessness, were often called on to apply muscle, money and mayhem to protect the interests of Jake's select list of clients. Jake always got the job done.

The rescue of Maddy had turned out to be an especially intractable task. Maddy had been kidnapped by slavers one night on a lonely road near her home about 45 miles outside of Knoxville, Tennessee. She had been kept in a basement dungeon on a farmstead in Georgia until collected by the men who had placed a special order for her. Well, not for her, really, but for someone just like her.

Maddy's misfortune was to be of such stature, body type and comeliness as to make her an exceptional candidate for the position of ponygirl. She was broad of shoulders, but not fat. She had long, strong legs. Her breasts were of the size and shape which were most admired. She had a graceful torso that slimmed down to an attractive waist. Her hips were prominent, but curved nicely to her thighs. Her face was pretty, but that was of no moment. For as a ponygirl, Maddy's face would never be seen.

Jake had been hired to find her. He and his team traced her first to a Georgia farmhouse and then to the basement of a warehouse in Elizabeth, New Jersey, the headquarters of the slaving ring. Jake and his team busted in one night and killed all of the slavers' crew save one. Feeney, the slim, but tough boss of the gang, had confessed at gun point before he too was sent to meet his maker, that they had been shipping slaves in airfreight containers by special jet to Kalikastan, a former Soviet republic located near the foothills of the Urals and nestled between the borders of Russia and the Ukraine. Maddy had been shipped on weeks ago. She was now in the hands of unknown buyers.

Burnham and Jake concocted a scheme where they would continue the stateside slaving operation using their own people as a way of gaining entry into the otherwise closed country. Once there, they would fall in with the criminal elements and find a way to track Maddy down. They did it, and Jake had found her. Now the question was how to get her out.

Jake felt himself coming, and Jackie, one of his favorite fucks, sensed it.

"Come on baby! Give me your cum! Fuck me baby! Fuck me!" she yelled as she locked him in tighter with her strong, sleek legs, drawing her long, sharp nails down his back, thrusting her hips hard to meet his.

It was all Jake needed. His whole body tensed as he felt himself begin to come. It was like a pool ball rolling of a table. You could see it rolling closer and closer to the edge. Then you saw it falling, tipping over, dropping inevitably to its destiny. And then it hit.

"Arrrrrrrgh!" Jake called out as his hot meat exploded. He could feel his juices flow down his manhood in mighty spurts. "Arrgh! Arrrrgh!" he cried.

"Yeah! Yeah! That's it Jake! Do it baby! Do it. Oh! I'm coming Jake! I'm coming! Don't stop baby! Don't stop!"

Jackie's body writhed underneath Jake. Her cunt grabbed his cock like a handshake. "Oh, yeah! Yeah!" Jackie cried out as her pleasure shot through her.

When Jake had exhausted his supply of hot, white spewm, he collapsed in Jackie's arms. She placed them around him and squeezed him tight. "Oh, Jake, what you do to me!" she said, laughing.

Either Jackie was one of the best whores in the world, or she had come like a freight train. Jake pulled his sticky cock from her dilated, soaking crevasse. He felt her body shudder as he vacated her womb.

Jake had known Jackie for years. She was his favorite whore. And one of his favorite people. He had pulled her out of big mess when she was just 18. Seems that a major league pimp with very good strong arm connections decided that she should work for him. Jake had found her one night on the streets of Chicago dressed only in a flimsy robe and crying her heart out. She had made her escape from the pimp, but had nowhere to go. She was deathly afraid that the pimp would track her down and make her suffer brutally for her impudence in seeking to flee a life of virtual sexual slavery. Normally, Jake didn't think that it was his job to save the world, but for once he decided to save a little piece of it. He 'persuaded' the dude to leave Jackie alone. After that, word on the street was that if you fucked with Jackie, you would have to deal with Jake. Jackie had never forgotten it.

Jackie rolled Jake off of her and rolled on top of him. She placed her enticingly plump lips on his chest and dragged her tongue across his skin. She placed her legs between his and, in an artful move, scooped up his flaccid but still tumescent cock between her thighs.

"I got you, Jake," she said.

"You got me, Jackie," he replied. "You got me good."

"I think I'll just hold you here until you're ready for another round, maybe help it along a little."

Jake ran his hand along Jackie's broad back. Jackie was a little big boned for a first class hooker, but she had flesh in all the right paces, and she knew how to use it.

Jake had not come to Chicago just to fuck Jackie. But he did come to see her. She had been first on his list when he thought of people that could solve his problem.

"I gotta talk to you Jackie," he said.

"Ahhh, Jake, we got time for business later. Let's fuck some more."

"Jackie, please, it's important."

"Okay, okay," the tall, dark brown lady of the night told him, disappointed. She released his manhood and rolled off him. "But I need a drink. I ain't talking business without a drink."

Jackie arose from the floor and loped across the room. She had a natural, animalistic grace. And she crossed the room in three steps. There was a bottle of Remy Martin on the bar together with two large snifters.

It was about 1 A.M. Jackie had given up the best time of the night to see Jake. She would do anything for Jake. He had told her over the phone that he had a problem and needed to talk to her. That was all he needed to say.

The tall, finely curved woman poured two hefty glasses of Remy and strode back to where Jake lay sprawled on the floor. Jake had rented the luxury hotel suite for them but they hadn't made it to the bed. Their clothes lay strewn around the room like they had undressed in the midst of a tornado. Jake took a glass from the young strumpet and sat up. He moved over so that he could lean up against the sofa. Jackie sat down with her legs crossed in front of him.

"Get my smokes from my jacket, will you, Jackie?" he asked the girl. She leaned over and pulled the tawny, herringbone, sports jacket towards her. In the right hand pocket was a pack of Lucky Strikes. She tossed the pack to Jake and he pulled one out and lit it. A cloud of blue gray smoke began to fill the room as he released his first, ceremonial toke.

"Jake," Jackie said. "You're stalling."

"Yeah, I'm stalling, honey. I just don't know if I'm doing the right thing."

"You ain't doing nothing yet, baby," Jackie replied. "Just tell me what you need and I'll go get it."

"It isn't something I need, Jackie," Jake explained. He took a long pull off the cognac and swilled it in his mouth before swallowing it. He looked directly at Jackie. "It's someone."

"I'm all yours, Jake. Anything you want."

Jake took a deep drag from his Lucky. The ash tray was on the glass coffee table next to him and he reached over and took it in his hand. "Listen, Jackie," he said, "if you do this thing, I don't want you doing it for me. It's got to be for you."

The attractive, young woman shifted her position. "Gimme one of them Luckies, Jake," she said. Jake threw her the pack. She lit one and took a deep drag. Her breasts rose and fell gently with her breath. It was a thing of beauty. Jake felt his little boy rise.

"Okay," the whore said. "What is it? Or do I have to guess."

Jake explained about Maddy's kidnapping. He told her that she had been taken to a country called Kalikastan, a former Soviet republic which now was more like Chicago in the twenties. Except there were no cops.

"The guys who run the place are mostly Russian gangsters. They control most of the illegal activities in Russia and the Ukraine. They have ties to criminal gangs all over the world."

"So what's this got to do with me?" Jackie asked.

"I'm getting to that," Jake answered. It was a difficult story to tell, almost unbelievable. But Jake had seen it with his own eyes, had been, and still was, knee deep in it.

"One of the things that they've done there is to revive certain ancient customs," Jake told her.

"You mean like royalty and stuff?"

"No, not royalty, slavery."

"Slavery? Are you kidding?" Jackie asked incredulously.

"No, I'm not kidding," Jake answered. "They kidnap girls from all over the world and make them sexual slaves."

"Sexual slaves? With chains and whips and stuff like that?"

"With stuff like that," Jake responded. "And it gets worse."

"What can be worse than slavery, Jake?"

"Well, do you know what a ponygirl is?"

"A ponygirl?"

"Yeah, a ponygirl."

Jackie laughed. "I seen some pictures of that kind of stuff on a website. You mean girls hauling around carriages, like horses or something?"

"It's no laughing matter, Jackie. I'm 100% serious. That's why Maddy was kidnapped, to turn her into a ponygirl."

"And she's a ponygirl now?"

"Right now," Jake answered. "Right this minute she's probably just getting up after spending the night all tied up in a barn. In a little while she'll go for a run. And sometime later, a man will hook her up to a carriage and make her haul him all around."

Jake poured into his throat the remainder of his cognac and stubbed out his cigarette. Jackie was looking at him like he was a man from Mars. "I still don't see what this all has to do with me?" Jackie said. She got up and went across the room to retrieve the bottle of Remy. Jake could not help but admire her tight, curvaceous ass, her long, sexy back. When she turned, she saw that he was staring at her. She smiled, a right, happy smile.

"I like the way you look at me Jake. It gets me all a tingle. What do you say we forget all this talking and get back to business?" With this, she undulated her hips and shook her enticing breasts.

"Honey, please, this is serious. Let me ask you a question. How long have you been hooking?"

"Hooking? Sheeit!" she replied as she sat down again in front of Jake, her legs crossed. "I started hookin' when I was 17, Jake. You know that."

"And before you started hooking you went to school and all that? You were a track star, weren't you?"

Jackie laughed. "That's right. My friends called me Ex-Lax because I was so fast. Then, well, let's just say I made some mistakes."

"How much money have you got saved up, Jackie?"

Jackie turned serious. She filled her snifter about half way with Remy and handed the bottle over to Jake. "Well, Jake," she said, "I got about 500 bucks that I made from a trick this afternoon."

There was a silence between them. Jake poured three fingers of Remy in his glass and lit another Lucky. After a few moments, Jake spoke again, softly. "You can't do this forever, Jackie. You know that."

Jackie looked up at him, her eyes were watering. She had a long, almost regal face. Her lips were plump and inviting. Her large, brown eyes were usually bold and unafraid. "Please don't do this Jake. It's my life. I don't want any kind of lecture from you."

"It's not a lecture, honey. You know that I wouldn't do that. But let me ask you another question. How would you like to make a million bucks?"

Jackie looked up at Jake, her eyes widened. "A million bucks? Nobody's going to pay me a million bucks for a couple of blow jobs, Jake."

"I know someone who will," Jake answered. "But it involves a little more than a couple of blow jobs. It would be very dangerous and you'd have to go through some very difficult things. But, if all works out at the end, you'll have a million bucks, tax free."

"Weeeou!" Jackie exclaimed. "Where do I sign up?"

"Wait a second, honey. You have to know what's involved."

"Jake," Jackie said, turning serious again. "I risk my life every day. I'm just waiting for the asshole john who's going to beat the shit out of me, stuff me in his trunk and then cut me all up into little bits. Or maybe he'll just strangle me. You asked me how long I can keep doing this? Well, right now I make $500 per hour and $2,000 a night. I'm at the top of the game. But in a year I'll be 23. After that, things'll start goin' downhill pretty fast. When I'm 30, I'll be working some street corner for $25.00 a fuck." Jackie downed half of her glass. Then she added, "If I live that long." She looked back at Jake. "I don't have to know, Jake. If you're involved, I know you'll protect me as best you can. And if something happens, well, that's the way it goes."

"I may not be able to protect you, Jackie. There are some really rough boys out there."

"But I know that if you can, you will, Jake. That's all that matters."

Jackie looked down for a moment and then back up at Jake. "Does this involve this ponygirl thing?"

"Yes," Jake answered. He told her about the ponygirl races and the big tournaments they have. He explained that Maddy had won the championship in her class and that the guy who owned her wouldn't sell her. She couldn't be snatched because the country was as tight as a drum and they wouldn't be able to get Maddy out.

"The set up is this," he told her. "If you agree, you'll be shipped to Kalikastan to become a ponygirl. You'll be taken to Mr. Burnham's estate where you'll be trained to race a ponygirl cart. We think that we can get this guy, Grobgy, who owns her, to put Maddy up in a stakes race. If he wins, he'll get some contracts that are worth millions of dollars. If he loses, we get Maddy."

Jackie thought about this for a moment. "And what's it like to be a pony girl and how long do I have to do it?" she asked.

"The answer to your second question is about five months. The answer to your first question is this. A ponygirl is considered to be property, just like an animal. And that's how you'll be treated. You won't be able to talk, because you'll be gagged all the time. You'll be whipped, probably almost every day. You'll sleep in a barn, all trussed up. And you'll wear a hood that hides your face. You won't look human and, for all practical purposes, you won't be human. Anybody who wants to can fuck you at any time, any way that they want."

"Well, that part's no problem," Jackie said. She was attempting a joke, but Jake could see that what he said had sunk in.

"But you'll be there Jake, won't you?"

"Jackie, once you say yes and we put this thing in motion, things will be out of my hands. Once you're in, you're in for the full ride. The only way you'll get out early is if Maddy dies, this guy Grobgy changes his mind and agrees to sell her or if he just won't go for the bait."

"Five months you said?"

"Five months," Jake replied. "It'll probably seem more like five years once you get started. Let me tell you Jackie, this thing'll be really rough. You don't have to do it. And don't do it if you think you're doing me a favor. It has to be because you've decided you want to take the risk. That you want a million dollars that bad."

"Oh, I want it, Jake. I want it."

Jackie paused and then asked, "Is there anything else I should know?"

Jake hesitated. How could he convey to her what life as a ponygirl was really like? He couldn't. Maybe he shouldn't have asked her. What if something went wrong? How could he forgive himself?

"Well, once you're there, at Burnham's estate, they'll tattoo you. One will be on your stomach, your lower belly. When they turn women into ponygirls, they tattoo the insignia of the estate on them. And they'll tattoo your name across your chest. Not your real name, but the name they'll give you."

The 22 year old whore stared at the floor for a moment. Then she put her glass aside and crawled over to Jake. She cuddled up to him and put her hand on his cock. "I'm going to do it, Jake. Now let's fuck."

CHAPTER TWO
LIFE IN THE PONY BARN

While it was 1 o'clock in the morning in Chicago, it was 9 A.M. in Kalikastan. It was time for the ponies to rise and shine and the grooms and trainers were making the rounds in the pony barn.

The sun was shining brightly over the vast estate owned by Axmail Grobgy, a former sergeant in the Soviet secret police. Grobgy had made his fortune in the years after the breakup of the Soviet Union through extortion, bribery, theft and murder. He now headed a multi-million dollar enterprise that handled a large portion of the contraband that flowed in and out of the former Soviet republics of Russia and the Ukraine. This fortune enabled him to be one of the preeminent owners and racers of ponygirls in the country.

There were a little over 30 ponies in Grobgy's main barn and another 10 in the auxiliary. The auxiliary barn was for the general purpose ponies, ones too old for racing but whose other physical qualities made keeping them around convenient. These ponies were usually used for leisurely rides around the estate and the neighboring countryside, for helping to train new pony girls to a cart or were being held for sale on the secondary market.

There were seven trainers and twelve grooms on staff, so not every ponygirl could go through morning processing at the same time. The ponies needed to be allowed to relieve themselves and then be fed, bathed and shaved. Every day, at the start of the day, before they were brought out of their stalls, each pony suffered a ritualistic shaving of her head and loins. This was a way of emphasizing the fact of the masters' total control of their bodily functions and to emphasize to them the loss of their human status. They did not look like humans, they could not act like humans, and therefore they were not, in fact, human.

Lightning, formerly known as Madeline Burnham, or Maddy, one of the prize ponygirls of the Grobgy estate, had awoken in her stall early this day. Even though it had been over for two weeks, her body clock was still on her racing schedule where she had been awakened at 7 A.M. every day. It was not easy for Lightning to determine what time of day it was when she woke. Although the morning light shown in directly through the skylights in the barn, at night the ponygirls slept with the Velcro flaps of their hoods down. No light came in through the ponygirl hood, and when Lightning awoke she was still in complete darkness.

The barn was quiet. She could hear the light snoring of the pony girl whose stall was next to hers. She didn't know which of the ponies it was. The only other one that she knew by name was Persephone, because she had been her racing partner for a little over three weeks in the racing season and they had spent some time training together. She had little contact with any of the others except during the footrace held every morning as a prelude to the day's activities. But there were so many of them and she got to see them only for brief periods of time.

Lightning could also hear the footsteps of the night watchman whose job it was to walk the rounds through the pony barn every night. It was a sound that Lightning dreaded. Every time that she heard the distinct, heavy tread of his heels striking the wooden floor of the barn, she imagined that it was someone coming for her, someone coming to awaken her from her slumber, remove her from her stall, in order to visit torment upon her body.

For it did happen. Twice over the last two weeks, Lightning had been shaken to awareness, brought out to the yard in front of the barn and beaten. She never knew who did it since she was kept blinded by her hood. No words were spoken, no indication given as to whether she was being punished for some misdeed or whether it was just on someone's whim. She had heard other ponies dragged out in the middle of the night too. She could hear their muffled sobs, suppressed by their thick, leather gags, when they were brought back in.

She was startled when she felt the strong hands unfastening the belts around her ankles and thighs. Pony girls slept lying on their backs, their arms imprisoned behind them, and their ankles and thighs strapped firmly together. Their collar and ankles were then be affixed to rings in the floor. Even asleep, a ponygirl had no right to volitional movement. She couldn't roll over, sit up, bend her knees. She slept cocoon-like, immobile until released.

When her collar and ankles were freed from their confinements, a hand seized the ring at the front of her collar and pulled her to her feet. She wore the standard ponygirl collar, made of hard plastic covered by a thick layer of soft leather. It was higher in front than in back, forcing the pony into a posture ideal for racing, her body bent forward, pulling her carriage or cart, her head pointed towards the track ahead.

As soon as she was brought to a standing position, Lightning knew that something was not right. Usually in the mornings she could hear the noise made by the other ponygirls and their attendants preparing for the day's events. But instead of the running of water, the shuffling of feet, the rattling of chains, she heard nothing. Dead silence. She stood stock still while a leash was affixed to the golden ring in her nose. She heard the creak of her stall door opening and then felt herself propelled forward.

She was not wearing her ponygirl boots. They did not sleep in them, but they wore them at all other times. Her bare feet slapped on the wooden floor of the barn. The heavy tread of boots preceded her. The ponygirl stalls were constructed in a kind of warren with a narrow corridor leading through them and Lightning found herself taken through several twists and turns before she achieved the barn door. It was already open and she was pulled through it.

It was cool outside from the nighttime air, but Lightning could feel the residual warmth of the harsh Kalikastan sun in the soft earth beneath her feet. Of course, Lightning didn't know that she was in Kalikastan. She didn't even know where Kalikastan was or had even ever heard of it. She only knew that the men spoke a harsh guttural language that she presumed to be Russian or Serbian or something. She knew that she was far away from home. She also knew, or thought that she knew, that no one knew were she was or could ever find her.

The frightened ponygirl was led to a heavy, seven foot tall post anchored in the dirt. She was frightened because nothing like this had ever happened to her before. Ponygirls thrived on routine. They had no control over their environment and so they liked things nice and familiar. Change often meant immersion in some new aspect of their dehumanized state that would work some new torture or abuse on them. They were usually right. Ponygirls' lives rarely got better. They often got worse.

As the front of her collar was affixed to a ring on the post, Lightning began to whine. She had been hooked to posts before and knew what it meant. When she felt one of her arms released from the strap that hung from the rear of her collar, her knees got weak and her stomach turned over. Her hands had been locked behind her literally almost ever since she had been kidnapped. They were rarely loosened.

When they were, it was usually so that a tormentor could have access to the tender skin of her back. That was the only explanation that Lightning could think of now.

Lightning's wrists were fastened to rings on the sides of the post, about two feet above the level of her head. The post was almost three feet around and Lightning's arms were spread well out of the way, leaving her back vulnerable and exposed. Hands took hold of her long, brown ponytail and twisted and curled it so that it could be pinned to the top of her hood. A strap went around her ankles and was then hooked to the post making it impossible for the ponygirl to dance and squirm to avoid the lash. It would land where it was aimed.

Although she knew that it would do no good, Lightning wanted to beg and plead for mercy. The gag in her mouth was in the form of a thick, leather plug that filled her oral cavity. It was attached to a thin, leather shield that covered her mouth and chin. All but the most violent screams and moans were suppressed by this device. Lightning knew that her even her most abject entreaties would emerge only as low, garbled murmurs.

Whoever it was that had brought the distraught ponygirl out in the middle of the night was in no hurry. After her securements were complete, Lightning heard the man step away. And then there was silence. Silence at night is different than silence in the day. Daytime silence is usually calming, peaceful. But silence at night is ominous, heavy. The fact that the dime sized eyeholes in Lightning's blue, Neoprene hood were covered meant that she could not even see the landscape around her painted in the soft, mellowing light of the moon, nor the hope inspiring points of light that were the stars.

At first, the night seemed truly silent. After a while, Lightning could hear the chirp of insects, a screeching of an owl echoing through the night. In her darkness, the sounds they made seemed amplified and terrible. She had no way of knowing how long she stood there, prepared for the whip. Her collar was affixed closely to the pole so that her large, naked breasts were pushed up against it. Although her hands were attached to the pole above her, her arms did not bear any of her weight. Having been rendered useless for many months, the muscles there had atrophied and were diminished and weak. Lightning had made it a habit, whenever she could, to flex her hands and fingers, clenching her fists tightly, to preserve some functionality there. But her upper arms were almost like dead weights and it would have been dangerous by now to force her to hang by them. When possible, dehabilitating injuries to ponygirls were avoided.

When Lightning heard the sound of boots returning, her heart skipped a beat. She had been agonizing over her impending dance with the whip. Some small part of her had begun to hope that she was wrong. But when the footsteps approached and stopped some distance behind her, she heard the unmistakable 'whooshing' sound of a switch being swung through the air.

The first blow struck the young ponygirl across the middle of her bare back. It burned like fire. Lightning's knees went weak and she uttered a pitiful cry. The second blow struck across her buttocks, tearing cruelly into her flesh. Her body shook in response and she struggled to free her collar from the pole, pulling at it futilely.

Each time that the whip did its fiendish work, Lightning's body shivered and trembled, scraping her tender breasts and thighs against the coarse wood of the pole. Again and again the whip struck her, randomly descending down to the sensitive skin on the backs of her shins or up to the backs of her thighs or to the top of her back across her shoulder blades.

Lightning cried and screamed in pain. She had been whipped many times. She would never get used to it. Her stomach turned and her heart beat loudly every time that she was secured in preparation for applying the bite of a lash against her body. It was no different now. Her assailant took his time, letting the impact of each blow subside before landing the next. As the burning pain of the blow lowered to mere excruciating discomfort, Lightning's mind would turn frantically to the next blow and where it might land.

There came a pause. Lightning cried and cried in dismal agony. The boots approached her and she felt her arms and collar released from the post. The belt binding her ankles to it was undone. Hard, rough hands grabbed her shoulders and turned her around. When she felt the back of her collar clipped to the post, the wretchedly unhappy ponygirl knew that more was to come.

When she was again in position, her hands above her and to the sides, her legs bound together to the post, her whipping resumed. Fire licked at her breasts, belly and thighs. The lashes felt like razors being dragged across her body. She wailed behind her gag and shook her featureless head in misery. Her body strained at its confines. There was no way to avoid or mitigate the blows. She could only stand and suffer.

After the last blow was struck, Lightning was left standing, her body wracked with her sobs. "What hell am I in?" Lightning asked herself miserably. "Is this my life, from now until I close my eyes, gratefully, for good?"

Lightning's legs had supported her, but now her knees sagged, causing pressure from her collar on her neck. She felt her airway close off and welcomed the opportunity to expire. But ponygirls are valuable animals and no owner or trainer would let one die without good cause.

A strong arm wrapped itself around Lightning's waist and lifted her torso up, taking the weight off of her collar. Her arms were released from the pole and then her ankles. Slowly, the man let her body fall to the ground. Lying supine on her belly, Lightning felt her arms being reaffixed to the long strap that led from her collar down her back. The ground, although still warm from the day's heat, was cooler than the lacerations on her skin and felt soothing. Strangely, she was at peace. Her torture was done. She had survived.

The unknown man let Lightning lie undisturbed in the dirt for some time. She heard the striking of a match and a deep sigh from the man as he inhaled the first smoke from his cigarette. His presence lurked over her but seemed far away, almost in another universe. Lightning was in a world of her own. She was absorbing her experience, filing it away amongst the other terrors and tortures she had endured. It had not been the worst, but it had been close. It was just one more step further away from who she once was and to whom she knew she would never return. How could one go back to normal life? How would she learn to speak again, to move from place to place without instruction, to decide on her own when to eat, to defecate, to sleep? How would she greet her fellow creatures? Would anyone ever treat her as a person again?

As her consciousness of the world around her returned, Lightning wondered what she had done during the day to justify this punishment. If she only knew, she would correct it. But in fact, she had done nothing wrong except be who she was, a dehumanized female who needed to have every spark of personhood driven from her.

The night time whippings were administered randomly and for the express purpose of maintaining a certain level of terror for the ponygirls, especially for the ones returning to the pony barn after racing season, as was Lightning. Their days were otherwise regulated mostly by routine and it didn't do for any of them to get too comfortable. If a ponygirl performed all of her required tasks with alacrity and enthusiasm, she might avoid contact with a whip for days at a time. It was generally believed that it was important to keep ponygirls' familiarity with the whip fresh.

This morning, shortly after awakening, Lightning heard the fearsome, deliberate sound of boot heels striking the wooden floor. Since her vision was blocked, she could not tell if she had awoken in the middle of the night or near morning. When she heard the footsteps approach the door of her stall, her muscles tightened and she began to sweat. She held her breath until the footsteps passed. Then, spared for the moment, she relaxed and thanked providence for her deliverance.

When the footsteps had passed her stall, Lightning listened carefully for the telltale signs of daybreak. There was a rooster on the estate and every morning at sunrise he would announce the auspicious event. There were certain morning birds that she was able to hear through the wooden walls of the barn, sounds normally blocked out by the myriad sounds of human or pony activity during the day. It was that sound that first told Lightning it was morning today and that she no longer had to dread the sound of the fearsome footsteps. It was morning, and soon she would face the other hazards of the day, but not this particular one.

CHAPTER THREE
A PONY IS READIED FOR THE DAY

Lightning welcomed the sounds of the grooms and trainers entering the barn. She had lain docile and helpless for what seemed like several hours since she had awoken. Her thoughts had drifted over the events of the past few months. She was trying to pinpoint the time that her humanity had come to an end. Because she no longer thought of herself anymore as a human woman.

Was it when she was kidnapped and her right to speak was taken away? Was it when she was first induced to issue garbled and muffled screams and pleas for mercy when she was whipped or to sigh and moan when she was brought to exquisite, unwilling orgasm by her masters and lords? Or was it when her head and loins were first shaved, her hands pinned behind her, a ponygirl hood applied? She had once had a name, Madeline, but that was long ago. Madeline was dead. Her name now was Lightning, or 'Molnya', in Russian, as was emblazoned across her chest tattooed in two inch high, blue, Cyrillic letters. Was it then, when she was renamed?

When she first arrived at the Grobgy estate she had been raped by the man who she understood to be her owner. It was her first use as a ponygirl, although at the time she did not know that was what she had become. She had been bound, gagged and hooded, her vision restricted to what she could see through tiny slits, not a person, just a body. Was it then, when her owner leered into her eyes as he drove her to orgasm and pumped his seed into her womb, that she became unhuman?

Had she still thought of herself as human after her trainer, she did not know his name, had dressed her in full ponygirl regalia and then whipped her unmercifully for the first time? It had certainly made her eager to obey.

She remembered well the first day that she had been harnessed to a cart. She had cried when the leather straps were applied to her and she was fastened to the yokes. She was coupled with an older, more experienced pony and handed over to the cruelties of a young, blond boy who taught her to obey the dictates of her reins and punished her severely when she faltered.

She had seen the other ponygirls pulling carriages and carts of all descriptions before that, but had never fully comprehended her fate. Her training until then had consisted of running around a little ring, the ring on the leather shield on her face attached by a chain to a rotor driven arm. Around and around the circle she would run, hour after hour, her legs screaming for relief, her mind reeling with humiliation and despair. When the blond haired boy had climbed up into the cart and flicked the reins and she had dutifully, obediently, stepped forward, she felt that she had left everything that she ever was behind. Was that when she had lost her humanity?

Lightning began to cry. What right did these men have to do this to her? What twisted sense of what was good, fair and just propelled them? Or did they have any? Did they have wives, children, sisters, mothers? Did they have any friendliness or warmth in them? If they did, why did they not have any for her? But she knew the answer. Somewhere along the line they had stopped thinking about her as a real person. She was shaped like a person, had the body parts of a person, but she did not function like a person. She had no will. She had no identity. She had no face.

And then there was the sex.

At first, Lightning had rebelled and recoiled at the unconsented to use of her body. When she was kidnapped, she had been forced at the point of a cattle prod to suck the prick of the old man who had captured her. When she had been in that dungeon that they took her to next, with the long line of cages filled with forlorn, young women and the strange, black haired girl who fed and cleaned her, her mouth had been raped by the thin, cruel looking man who seemed to be in charge. Then she had been raped while laying on a hay bale by her owner in front of god knew how many men laughing and cheering him on. He had forced her to come and she hated herself for it.

After that, the use of her body accelerated rapidly. She did not know how many men raped her that first night, tied to the rail in her stall, their stiff pricks ravaging her front and rear. Some of those men had made her come, writhing and moaning unwillingly. And then there was her trainer, he had taught her a new way of pleasure. He had taught her to come with a hard cock up her ass and nothing else. Now, it was like she had two cunts, and either could be used to drive her to pleasure.

And her mouth; it had only two uses. She was permitted to use it to eat. At mealtimes she would bend over a bowl and slurp up whatever gruelish fare they had prepared for her. And she better eat it all, or else. But it was the other use of her mouth that was more important. From the first day, when her trainer beat her almost senseless, she had assiduously obeyed any command to suck a cock. At first, she felt demeaned and humiliated that they would use her this way, forced to her knees, focused on the task of bringing the man pleasure and no other. Each time, she felt the dominance of the man and her own helplessness. She felt soiled each time a man shot his white load into her mouth or down her throat.

But eventually she had seen the truth. She was a slut and a whore and loved the feel of a hard cock in her mouth. She felt rewarded when her trainer signaled her to her knees and opened his pants. Her whole body tingled and her cunt burned as she worked the stiff wand of flesh with her lips and tongue. Her mind clouded over when she took the throbbing meat in her throat. And she often came when she felt the hard, hot cock discharge, felt the warm splash of the cum in her mouth, felt the pulsing of the cock on her lips. When had that transformation occurred?

Soon, the groom or a trainer would come to her stall. She would be given her morning ablutions and shaved. She would be allowed to eat. And then she would be stroked to orgasm. She would spread her legs and passively accept the manipulation of her sex until her body shuddered and her mind reeled with each contraction of her wet pussy. Occasionally, her attendant would take advantage of her exposed and lubricated state to slide his hard meat into her and achieve his own pleasure. Even now, as Lightning thought about it, her slit began to moisten and her blood began to burn.

She needed it now. Needed it every day. She needed it every hour, every minute. A stroke of a hand on her rear, the sound of a zipper being lowered, the order to open her mouth to receive someone's hard rod, was enough to make her blood run hot, to make her gush below.

Finally, Lightning heard the noise of the men entering the barn. Doors were opened, chains unleashed, faucets run. Her own stall door opened and she felt herself being released. Who would it be today, the somewhat shy, red headed boy or the heavy set blond one with the thick fingers and the smirking grin? Would she finally see her trainer today?

Anton Drabik, a former Red Army colonel and Lightning's trainer, had fucked her the night of the celebration of the championship that she won. Actually, the celebration was for the fact that the estate had won the overall ponygirl racing championship, but Lightning could not know that. She only knew that all of the racing ponies had been driven in a parade before a crowd of fancy dressed guests, male and female, and that after, her owner, her trainer and her driver, a cruel, dwarfish man who had abused and tormented her, late at night had come to her and used her and beat her in their own twisted idea of how her victory should be celebrated.

She wore a golden medal on her collar as evidence of her feat. She could move her head and hear it jungle. She wore it with pride. She had beaten the best. It was hard and she had dug down deep inside herself to win it. She had wanted it more than anything else she had ever wanted in the world. Somehow, she felt that this redeemed her, set her apart. She was not like all the other ponies. She was different. She was a champion. You could look it up.

She had expected that her trainer, whose name she did not know, would see her the next day, if only to heap more abuse on her. The last time she had been in his custody he had beaten her severely, raped her cruelly, all the behest of his jealous lover, a beautiful black haired woman. After that, she had been removed from the pony barn and kept in the custody of her drivers. She was out of bounds for use by anyone else but them and her owner. When the Spring Tournament was over, she was returned to the pony barn. But he had not come. She had not seen him. And this morning, it was not he who opened the panels over her tiny eyelets in her hood.

It was another of the trainers. He was a broad shouldered man of medium height. He had close cropped, black hair, a ruddy face and large, powerful hands. He was dressed in a black t-shirt and work pants with heavy boots. As Lightning looked up at him from her prone position, he smiled, a wry, amused smile, and pinched her breast hard with his finger and thumb. He kept pressing until he had wrenched a moan of pain from the helpless female. He muttered something unintelligible to her in Russian and then pulled her to her feet by her collar.

The first order of business was to let the ponygirl relieve herself. The trainer placed a specially designed chamber pot under Lightning and she bent her knees and hovered over it. When she was done, the trainer cleaned her, washed his hands and then presented her with her breakfast. Lightning knelt before the bowl and waited for the trainer to remove her gag. The ponygirls were fed a carefully planned and balanced diet. Unfortunately, it was usually pureed into a soupy gruel. It did not matter whether the ponies enjoyed eating it or not. It was their job to eat it. The gruel also included the medical necessities to eliminate pregnancies and menstrual flow. The ponies were therefore available for intercourse at any time.

Lightning bent her face to the ceramic bowl and began to lap up her morning repast. The trainer linked her collar to a hook in the wall next to where he had placed the bowl and left the stall to perform other duties. When he came back, about 15 minutes later, Lightning had consumed her meal and was waiting patiently on her knees for her mouth to be wiped and her bowl removed. Sitting alone in her stall, her gag on the floor next to her, her blue covered, featureless head held erect, Lightning often was tempted to cry out her protests at her treatment and her fate. She was able to curb this impulse because of the certainty of extreme punishment (talking was about the worst offense that a ponygirl could commit) and the fact that she had watched the punishment of a ponygirl who had not.

All of the ponies had been called out to witness the torment of the offender. No announcement was made as to why they were assembled. They all knew that one of them had crossed a terrible line. The pony who had sinned had cried out in words that Lightning did not recognize. But they were words and for that crime the pony had to pay.

The ponies all obediently knelt in the dust outside the barn while the offending pony was dragged out and brought to a steel frame that sat outside. A harness was strapped around her body and attached to the frame above. She twisted and turned to avoid being hung from the frame, but to no avail. She was beaten terribly for almost an hour. The men took turns landing terrible blows against her defenseless body with a fierce multi-thonged whip, on her breasts, her belly, her thighs and back. Her terror was obvious as her muffled moans and cries of anguish could be heard through the gag that covered the lower half of her face. But nothing could be discerned from looking at her. All that could be seen was an expressionless mask of blue.

When the men finished beating her with the whip, the pony was allowed to swing forlorn and lifeless from the frame for several minutes. Like all the ponies, she had long, graceful legs and lovely twin orbs that, despite their weight, rode prominently on her chest. She had a long, brown ponytail reaching to her waist. One of the men came up and captured the pony's legs and belted them together at the ankles while another curled the long ponytail and pinned it to her hood. The sound of her anguished pleas, not words, just sounds, rent Lightning's heart. She prayed that she would never be mounted to the frame for public discipline.

The men resumed her punishment. They started in on her with long switches that left angry red marks wherever they landed. Two men worked at her at once and she suffered a steady stream of blows. Soon her legs, her breasts, her whole body, even her useless arms were covered by long trails of red. She screamed and moaned and writhed frantically, her body swinging in the air.

A large crowd of men had gathered to watch. When the first two men were done, two more men emerged from the crowd armed with riding crops. The sound of the crops striking the anguished pony's flesh was sickening. They belabored her thighs, front and back and lower legs, her arms. One of the men brought out a long strap. He fixed one end around the strap that bound the pony's ankles and tied the other one off at the top of the frame just high enough so that the soles of the pony's feet were rendered vulnerable. In a slow, steady cadence, the men struck the soles of the pony's feet with thick wooden rods. The pony's moans were long and anguished.

At this, the pony was lowered to the ground and the harness was removed. While the pony laid moaning and crying in the dirt, straps were tied onto her two ankles. She was then quickly hauled back up onto the frame, her legs spread, her blue clad head hanging towards the ground. Her arms were unfastened from behind her back and tied to a weight that pulled them straight. Then the men with the switches returned and began their work again.

A sea of blank, blue heads watched the proceedings with terror, mesmerized by the vicious violence. They had all experienced the lash, the riding crop. But few had ever seen any of the ponies tortured in anger. Most of their beatings were meant to be instructional, or were inspired by lust. The terrible vision of the masters' ire was devastating.

When the men were done tormenting her with the various whips and clubs, the pony was released. She fell to the ground in a clump. Her almost lifeless body was dragged to a nearby post and, after her wrists had been reaffixed behind her back, her body was strapped to it firmly. A trainer removed her stifling gag and pried open her mouth. A pincer seized her tongue and pulled it out.

Another trainer laid a hot poker upon it. The pony had stood there docilely while she was strapped to the pole. She now came wide awake. Her body stiffened and strained at its confinements. Her head was held firmly by two of the trainers, but they had to struggle to keep it still. She screeched and wailed at the pain louder than poor, frightened Lightning had ever heard before.

The unfortunate pony was made to stand there all day with her scalded tongue hanging out of her mouth as an example for all the other former women. No gag was needed to prevent words since her tongue had swollen so that only a weak blubbering sound could emerge.

And so Lightning always fought back any urge she had to speak while the gag was out of her mouth. She knelt silent and obedient. And all the other ponies did likewise.

When the trainer returned, he took away the bowl and ordered her, by a motion of his hand, to turn away from him, her face to the wall. Kneeling behind her, he removed her hood and collar and then began to wash her face and neck with a special, creamy soap designed to reduce any irritation to the skin and render it soft and pliant. Lightning knelt with her face turned away from the trainer, minimizing his view. No one looked into the face of a ponygirl. After a soothing lotion had been applied, the trainer shaved her head, scraping away a lathering of soap and any growth that had taken place over the prior 24 hours. All but the long strands of hair that constituted Lightning's ponytail were removed.

Although Lightning mourned the loss of her personality, ironically, she had grown to be ashamed at the thought of showing her male groomers her face. She knew what she had become and only her total anonymity allowed her psyche to tolerate it. With her face exposed, if only for a minute or two while she was groomed, Lightning regained some of her identity, could be recognized. But it was over quickly and, after the man threaded her ponytail through a fresh, clean hood, Lightning's face was covered once again.

After replacing her gag, the trainer pushed Lightning's torso back against the wall. He did not have to tell her what to do next. She spread her legs and raised her knees. She slid down slightly so that she could present her upturned loins to him. As he applied the lathered soap to her lower belly and her labial lips, Lightning's slit began to moisten. The shaving of her sex and all its environs was a prelude to her morning delight.

When the trainer finished carefully scraping away the tiny stubs of hair that had grown since yesterday, he toweled her off and applied a soothing cream to the shaved areas. Lightning stared up at him from behind her tiny eye holes expectantly. He grinned at her and reached out and pinched her nipples gently. They were already stiff with desire. He ran his hands down her torso and over the inside of her thighs. Lightning sighed in anticipation of his touch as he moved his hands down to the tender lips that lay astride her now leaking sex. The man's hands were hot on Lightning's cool skin. He placed the palm of his right hand on her belly and then drew his thick, fat thumb up the length of her slit. The digit easily split Lightning's engorged lips and entered her yearning crevasse. She felt the thumb inside her as he stroked the sensitive roof of her sex. Drawing his thumb out, he passed it lightly over the bud at the apex of her cleft, spreading her pungent, sticky moisture there.

Lightning lay back against the wall, moaning, her thighs beginning to shake, her breasts hot and tight with blood. The man slowly and almost tenderly fucked her with his thumb, easing himself in and out, drawing little circles around and on her hard clit.

Lightning's breathing was becoming more and more shallow as the thumb excited her. She closed her eyes and let the pleasure of the man's caresses, surprisingly languorous and gentle for so hard a man, wash over her. Then she heard the sound of the man's zipper being lowered. He had pulled it down with his free hand and was now pulling Lightning's legs towards the center of the stall so that she lay flat on the floor. He climbed between her thighs and placed the hot head of his stiffened manhood against her engorged lower lips. Slowly, almost torturously, he slid himself inside the panting and moaning ponygirl.

Lightning raised her hips to meet the man's cock and spread her legs wide. She sighed deeply as it filled her. She did not care what this man may have done to her on other days, at other times; she did not care what he might do to her later. Now, she wanted him to drive her to completion,

The impassioned ponygirl reveled in the long, hard slow thrusts that the man made into her hot, tight tunnel. Her body trembled as the first waves of a mild, rolling orgasm flowed through her. Her pussy contracted around the man's cock and he moaned in turn. It was his signal to begin to thrust into the ponygirl in earnest. His cock began to plunge back and forth into Lightning's sheath faster and faster. Lightning's blood began to rise again, it had never really cooled, and she felt the impending hard, passionate release coming on. "Mmmmmmm! Mmmmmmmmmmm!" she moaned as the stiff meat pushed her past the crest. Her pussy devolved into hard, pleasure giving throbs. She felt her inner self tightly squeeze the man's organ as her body shuddered at each exquisitely pleasurable contraction.

The man grunted and she felt his hot fluids empty into her. His pulsing meat drove her on and on and on until finally, as his forces dwindled, her spasms began to calm. The man had covered the pony's body with his and the two lay there for several moments, each of them luxuriating in the floating world of spent passion. The man moved first, sliding his softening prick from Lightning's lush hole.

The satisfied trainer stood and put away the shaving kit. He reached down and, circling a thick finger in the ring on the front of Lightning's collar, drew her to her feet. Her shower was next and the washing of her pony tail. There was a hose attached to the spigot with a soft, rubber shower head on it. The trainer adjusted the temperature of the water and then turned Lightning around so that her back was to him. Lightning knew the routine. She brought her head back so that the man could wet her long skein of hair without soaking her hood. When it was wet, he shampooed it and then rinsed out the soap. He applied a cream rinse that would make the pony tail soft and shiny. After he washed out the cream rinse he dried the tail, brushed out any knots and applied the bands that kept it gathered and tail-like.

Lightning's body was next, and the man ran the head of the hose over her torso and then soaped her body thoroughly. Lightning was, as usual, still slow and befuddled from her moments of passion, and the feeling of the warm water running all over her body gave her small, residual twinges of pleasure. She felt the strong hands of the man as he massaged her breasts, cleaning them carefully, pulling at the stiff nipples. He soaped the entrance to her womb and her rear and rinsed them, lingering until the ponygirl moaned again. He washed her legs and her feet.

Lightning stood still as the trainer dried her body with a large towel. He then knelt and held out each of her pony boots as she stepped into them. He tied them up snugly and brought her to her feet. The former human female stood naked before him, hands locked behind her, staring through the tiny holes in her hood, awaiting his instructions. She had a graceful, desirable body and the trainer gazed at it appreciatively.

Lightning knew what he would do next, but ponies were never to anticipate orders. He seized her heavy breasts with his hands and stroked them until the pony's fat nipples were hard again. He laughed as he released them and turned her around and pushed her body up against the long rail that ran across the stall near its back. Lightning's waist was tied to the rail by a leather strap. The man knelt, and, after nudging the pony's thighs apart, hooked her boots to rings in the floor. He got up, ducked under the rail and extended a light chain from the wall in front of the ponygirl and affixed its end to her golden nose ring. He carefully pulled the chain tight through a hook in the wall and fastened it off.

The fed and groomed pony stood with her legs apart, her belly hard up against the rail and her torso tilted forward, forced towards the wall by the chain that led to the ring in her nose. Her breasts hung free from her chest and swayed gently as the pony adjusted her body to its positioning. The trainer ducked back under the rail and, before he departed, ran his finger along the length of her exposed slit from behind. Lightning shuddered at the touch. The man laughed. He let the stall door slam as he left.

CHAPTER FOUR
A KILLER MAKES A MOVE

Anton Drabik was, while Lightning was being prepped and handled prefatory to another day as a ponygirl, making himself a cup of coffee. He had not been to see Lightning for the last two weeks because he was taking care of some business for his boss, Axmail Grobgy. Drabik's other profession, besides being an experienced and valuable ponygirl trainer, was dealing death. He had left the Grobgy estate with a list. This was his last stop.

He had been waiting in the small country house outside of Rostak in the Ukraine the night before when his target and his young, beautiful girlfriend, had come home after an evening of partying. When they came in, he was sitting in a living room chair. The pair blanched when they saw him. The man, a small link in the chain of Grobgy's drug distribution network, had been short in a number of his transmittals of cash to the upper links in the chain and the conclusion had been reached that he was skimming. To make matters worse, he had been discovered to be free-lancing, that is, moving product on his own, product not bought from Grobgy.

Drabik forced the young girl, she seemed about 20 or so, at pistol point to tie off her boyfriend's hands behind his back. She was crying and her tears caused her mascara to run in little black rivulets down her face. When she had accomplished her task, Drabik placed his pistol in his shoulder holster and checked the bindings. He then had the girlfriend kneel, and he fixed her pretty, thin wrists behind her back. She had short, black hair cut evenly around her head like a pageboy. She was wearing a short, glossy, red miniskirt and a glittery gold lame blouse. Her legs were thin and alluring. Her lips were painted bright red and pursed in fear as she wondered whether she would outlive the night.

The boyfriend had been speaking rapidly, asking Drabik why he was here, protesting his innocence of any wrongdoing, offering money, his girlfriend, anything, to be spared. Most people in the business knew who Drabik was. A visit from him was a death warrant.

Drabik ignored the pleading man and placed a strip of duct tape over the mouth of the girl. She had not said a word since she and her boyfriend had entered, but why take the chance? One asshole begging and pleading for his life was enough. He looped tape around the girl's ankles several times and then pushed her to her stomach. He taped her hands to her ankles.

The boyfriend had quieted now, but was crying and blubbering. "Where's the money?" Drabik asked him.

"I'll get it, I'll get it! Please don't kill me, please!" the man answered fearfully. Drabik's response was to apply a strip of duct tape to the man's mouth.

"Get up and go get it." Drabik ordered.

The man rose from his knees and led Drabik upstairs. A few moments later the two came down. Drabik was carrying a leather attaché case full of cash. He had planned his next act carefully. He motioned the man into the kitchen with his gun. There was a walk-in pantry in the kitchen with no windows. He indicated for the man to get inside. Once the man had crossed the threshold, Drabik's pistol jumped twice. 'Pop! Pop!' The pistol spoke, its noise muffled by the silencer attached. The man fell forward, two holes in the back of his skull. His knees hit first and then his body pitched to the floor. Drabik closed the door to the pantry and returned to the living room.

The girl, who had heard the muted but still unmistakable sound of the shots, was sobbing when he entered the room. Drabik went to the bar and poured himself a scotch. He sat back in his chair, his eyes on the delightful and enticing body of the female as he drank. He had planned on sleeping here tonight. That's why the man's body was left in the pantry, so that any prying eyes in the morning wouldn't see his corpse. Drabik had known that the dead man probably wouldn't come home alone, but hadn't yet decided what to do about the girlfriend.

The posture of the girl, her legs bent back to her bound wrists, caused her flimsy red skirt to ride high on her thighs. Drabik could see the beginning of the delicious curves of her ass. Like many modern girls, she wore no panties but, instead, a narrow, scanty thong, and so her ass cheeks were bare. She had stopped sobbing, but was looking at Drabik with wide open, doleful eyes. She had small, firm breasts that were mashed underneath her.

Well, he was staying the night anyway. Why not have some diversion?

The killer rose from his chair and swallowed the rest of his scotch. He still had his long barreled pistol in his hand and the girl uttered a cry as she saw him get up. Drabik walked over to her, unfastened her wrists from her ankles and then freed her legs.

"Get up," he told her.

The girl started sobbing again, but obediently rose to her feet, her hands still bound behind her.

"Do you want to live?" Drabik asked her.

The girl nodded her head frantically.

"Then do what I say. I'm going to fuck you and you better be good."

Drabik motioned for the girl to ascend the stairs. He followed behind her. As he rose up the staircase, he could see the tops of the back of the girl's thighs from beneath her skirt. He looked forward to getting in between them.

When they reached the bedroom, Drabik had her stand by the foot of the large, plush bed while he undressed. When he was naked, he turned her around and undid her wrists.

"I want to see you strip, cunt, slowly. Give me a show," he told her.

The girl nodded her understanding and once Drabik had settled himself on the bed, leaning on some pillows against the headboard, she began to nervously pull her gold lame blouse over her head.

"No, no, you stupid cunt!" Drabik yelled. "Move your hips, dance, make me horny."

The girl nodded her eagerness to comply. Her mouth was still covered by the tape.

Slowly, she began to move her hips to some silent music in her head. She closed her eyes and, turning her back, showed Drabik her pretty little ass, moving it back and forth. She slid her hands down her torso like she had seen them do in the movies and rubbed her tight rear cheeks seductively. Still swaying, she reached her hands behind her and slowly began to pull her blouse upwards.

Drabik's cock began to get hard as he watched the girl reveal her naked back to him. Her hips swayed invitingly. She wore no bra. When the blouse was bunched at her neck, she turned slowly as she pulled it over her head. When her head emerged, she was looking directly at Drabik. Drabik was no one's idea of an Esquire man. Although his body was muscular and fit, he had a fearsome face and a long scar along one cheek. His eyes were set back in his head and were dark and piercing. He had short, but not close cropped, black hair. He had the pistol in his hand as he watched the girl's show.

He could see her shudder with fear as she slowly lowered her blouse from her chest. Her breasts were tea cup sized, but firm and with long pointed nipples. Her skin was pale and set off her blood red areolas well. The girl tossed the blouse aside, her eyes filled with tears. She put her hands over her head and twirled slowly for her tormentor. She kept up the swaying beat with her hips as she turned.

Drabik was hard now and beginning to get impatient. "Get on with it," he ordered her churlishly. The girl recoiled at his deep, gravelly voice. She loosened the zipper on the side of her bright red skirt and then slowly lowered it. She was wearing suede sandals with large, thick heels. It took some difficulty to get her skirt over her feet, but she managed to do it without falling. She was wearing a bright red thong to match her skirt. Her tummy was tight and sloped gracefully to her loins. Her thighs were well toned but not muscular. The girl turned around twice, swaying her hips and presenting her soft, pale rear globes to the man. After the second turn, she locked her thumbs in the waistband of the thong and slowly pulled it down over her hips. It was somewhat more difficult than her skirt to get over her sandals and it caught on one of the heels, almost causing her to fall on the floor. But she maintained her balance and was able to remove it and toss it aside.

The girl now stood still, naked, not sure what to do next. She wrapped her arms around her chest and then, thinking better of it, let them fall to her sides. Her sex was surrounded by a finely trimmed, black bush, small enough to be hidden by the narrow part of her thong. Drabik looked at it hungrily. "Now, come here," he ordered.

Hesitatingly, the girl climbed onto the bed. Drabik ordered her to lie down and then retrieved the roll of tape he had brought upstairs with him and tossed on the side table when he undressed. The girl was laying face down and he grabbed one leg and bent it back. He ran the tape around the girl's ankle and then joined her wrist to it. He did the same for the other wrist and ankle. He rolled her to her back.

The girl laid there, her thighs spread, her knees up, her hands bound to her ankles. Drabik pushed her thighs wider apart and placed himself between them. The girl emitted a small whine behind the tape over her mouth. Drabik looked up at her and smiled. Her wrinkled brow, framed by her short, dark hair, expressed her anguish. "You better be good," he told her ominously. The girl's eyes widened and she nodded. Teardrops fell from the corner of her eyes.

Drabik moved forward and, bending over, placed his head between the girl's tender, white thighs. She shuddered as he drew his tongue the length of her slit and began to worry the hooded nubbin at its top. His hands were on her thighs, moving them wide apart and up. He traced the outline of the gap between the girl's labial lips three times slowly, each time working it on and around the hardening bud at the top. The girl moaned as he plunged his long, thick tongue inside her moistened hole.

The fearsome assassin supped to his content at the girl's cleft, teasing her clit with his teeth, fucking her with his tongue. She was breathing heavily and her thighs were conveying an urge to come together to trap the pleasuring head between them. This was Drabik's signal to mount the impassioned girl. He rose and, edging himself forward, placed his rock hard cock between the girl's soft, engorged lower lips. The crevasse welcomed him, pulling tight against his meat as it slid down its length. The girl moaned again and her thighs clamped against Drabik's hips. Slowly, Drabik worked his prick back and forth, driving the young, pretty girl to moan and sigh. Her eyes were shut and Drabik pressed their lids open with his thumbs. Staring into her frightened, yet lustful eyes, he asked her, "You're not dead yet, are you?"

The girl issued a cry, muffled by the tape over her mouth, and began to thrust her hips against the hips of her invader. He felt her tighten the muscles inside her, narrowing her channel, increasing Drabik's pleasure. He seized one of her nipples with his lips and sucked on it hard, causing the girl to moan and writhe underneath him. She was fucking him back wildly now and their bodies were slapping together. "Oooh! Ooooh! Oooh!" she called out as her crises came upon her. Her pussy pulsed and contracted as she came, squeezing Drabik's meat. He felt his juices flowing and then he came, shouting, "Ahhhhhrgh!" as he pumped his hot seed into the girl's shuddering belly. Their bodies rocked and pummeled each others' as wave after wave of pleasure went through them. The girl raised her bound ankles and pressed them against Drabik's rear, in an effort to consume him with her lower mouth. Her hands twisted and turned next to them in their bindings.

When Drabik was finished, he pulled himself from within the girl. Her chest was still rising and falling rapidly as she tried to catch her breath, her nostrils flaring as she sucked in air through her nose. Drabik knelt between her knees watching her until her body calmed. Her eyes had been closed, but now she opened them to behold her executioner leering at her flesh.

"Not bad, cunt," Drabik told her. "Maybe I'll let you live until morning. Would you like that?"

Tears filed the girl's eyes and she nodded earnestly. "Okay, I'm going downstairs for a moment. If you have moved an inch, when I come back, I'll do you right there and then, got it?"

Having observed the girl's piteous, nonverbal assent, Drabik raised himself from the bed. He took his pistol with him as he descended the stairs. His purpose was to retrieve the scotch and once he had the bottle and a glass in his hand he quickly went back upstairs to the bedroom.

The girl was lying there as ordered. He placed the glass on the side table and poured himself two fingers. He sat down on the bed next to the girl and idly played with her sloppy pussy as he sipped his drink. She was pretty and Drabik was not one to waste good female flesh. He could drop her off at Mikhail's tomorrow. He had a favor to ask and he was sure that Mikhail could use her.

Having made his decision, Drabik pulled the girl down the bed and rolled her to her knees. He then got back on the bed and lay against the headboard. He spread his thighs wide and told her, "Come here." The girl crawled forwards on her knees until she was between his thighs, shuffling her bound ankles and wrists at the same time. He ripped the tape from her mouth abruptly, causing her to gasp with pain. "Suck my cock," he told her. "And make a good job of it. If you're a good cocksucker, maybe I'll take you along with me tomorrow when I go." He wasn't going to kill her, but she didn't have to know that. The pretty, frightened, young girl mewed with fear as she bent her head down to capture Drabik's flaccid cock. She seized it between her ruby red lips and began to suck the hardened wand of flesh as if her life depended on it.

* * * * * * * * * * * * *

In the morning, Drabik searched the house and found the dead man's stash of heroin, about two ounces. No sense leaving it for the cops. He had seen that the girl had track marks on her arm and he pulled her works from the pretty, little gold purse that she had with her the night before. He ordered her to shoot up. "And make it a good one," he told her. He wanted her out for a long time.

She was sitting at the kitchen table nodding out as he drank his coffee. Drabik went out to the car with the dope and the money and tossed them into the trunk. He had parked it out back so it would not be seen. He gathered the girl's clothes and her purse into a plastic garbage bag and threw it in too. If the cops found no sign of the girlfriend, they would assume that she was in on the murder of her boyfriend and had absconded with the money and the dope. Their search for her would be cursory. Who cared about a murdered drug dealer anyway?

Drabik retrieved a can of gasoline from the trunk and went back inside. He spread its contents all over the living room. When he had finished he put the empty can back in the car and then brought the girl out and put her in the trunk. She was eminently pliable due to her injection. He hogtied and gagged her with the tape. She was naked, but still wore her high heeled sandals on her feet. Why bother dressing her? She wouldn't need clothes where she was going. He returned into the house and lit a gas soaked rag. When he tossed it into the living room, the room alit with a loud, 'whoosh!' and burst into flames. No sense leaving fingerprints and DNA for the cops.

Three hours later, he pulled into Mikhail's compound. It was surrounded by high walls and enclosed Mikhail's large house, a large garage and a barracks type building. There were several cars in the courtyard. Mikhail, a short, rotund man with a bushy, black beard came out to greet him.

"Anton, good to see you," he said.

"The goods are in the trunk along with a little gift I have for you," Drabik replied. The two men walked to the trunk and opened it. The girl had come out of her drugged stupor and looked up at the men fearfully with her big, doe like eyes.

"Ah, Drabik, you are a man for my own heart!" Mikhail exclaimed. "Get her out and let's see what she looks like." Drabik released the anxious girl's legs and pulled her from the trunk. Her eyes darted around nervously as she took in her new surroundings.

"She's a nice piece," Mikhail said. The girl stood there docilely but fearfully as he ran his hands over her small, firm, naked breasts and then over her hips and between her thighs. When he pinched her dainty nether lips, she squealed.

"Have you fucked her?" he queried the assassin. "As if I have to ask," he added, laughing.

"Of course," Drabik answered, a slight smile on his face. "Why not?"

The men laughed.

"I had some Turks here yesterday looking for some fresh pussy. I'll give them a call," Mikhail told Drabik. "But we'll wait a couple days," he said, smiling while he caressed one of the girl's pretty breasts.

A couple of Mikhail's men had gathered and he told them to bring the girl into the barracks. "Have some fun, but don't mark her all up," he told them. Drabik handed one of the men the dope he had gotten from the dead man's house and the bag containing the girl's clothes. The girl gave him one last frantic look as one of Mikhail's coarse looking men took her by the arm. "Say goodbye," the man said to her. Drabik watched as the pretty, naked girl was dragged away. "Well, you can't keep them all," he thought to himself.

"Come on inside," Mikhail said, interrupting his memories of the night before. "I'll get you some lunch."

After the two men ate and a pretty, young, blond woman dressed in a slender yellow thong and nothing else had removed the dishes, Mikhail asked Drabik, "Okay, what's the favor?"

Drabik reached into his pocket and withdrew a picture that had been taken off the digital security cameras at Grobgy's estate. "This guy calls himself Jake Barnes. He's an American and works for this other Americanski, Michael Burnham. Burnham has been licensed to operate in Kalikastan and he's brought a lot of bucks with him. Everybody's ga-ga over him. But this Barnes guy seems to me more than just a bodyguard type. They came to our estate for the championship celebration and I got a good look at him. I want to know who he is and what he's doing here."

"No problem," Mikhail replied. The young girl had come back into the dining room and was standing on the side, her hands behind her back and her eyes lowered. She had curly, shoulder length blonde hair and pretty, round breasts.

"Before you go," Mikhail asked him, nodding at the girl, "do you want to get laid?"

CHAPTER FIVE
A NEW ENTERPRISE

At the very time that Drabik was handing over custody of the pretty, black haired girl to Mikhail, five anxious, naked, young women knelt in the middle of a 30' x 30' room in the basement of the Burnham mansion. The floor was covered in a soft, maroon rug, but the walls were stark concrete colored by a thin coat of whitewash. Their knees were spread and their hands were locked together on the top of their heads, raising their bare breasts up into presentation position.

The women were staring straight ahead as if they had been commanded to do so, which they had. Three of the women had long, brown hair that descended down their backs. One had short blonde hair, close cropped with fancy little ringlets in the front where her bangs would be. The fifth woman had hair as black as coal and it descended to her shoulders in thick, wavy curls. All of the women were pretty, they all had curvaceous shapes and generous breasts, as if they had been selected specifically for these attributes. Behind the women were long, aluminum canisters open at the top.

In the room with the young girls were two rather cruel looking men, each carrying a short cattle prod. The room was locked and could be opened only by means of an electronic combination keypad on the wall. None of the women had the combination.

The men were sitting on comfortable chairs. They both wore dark black t-shirts and army style, camouflage pants. One, whose nickname was Ozzie, had his Ipod on and was nodding to the beat of one of his favorite songs.

He had a plastic bottle of Pepsi at his feet. The other, content to sit and watch to see if any of the girls broke position, all the while admiring their delicious charms, was called Lem, short for Lemenowski. They were all waiting.

Meanwhile, outside the room, a lean, bearded man known as Arcady Renko was guiding the multi-billionaire Michael Burnham down the stairs. They were chatting amiably.

"So when will the building be finished?" Burnham asked him.

"In about six weeks," the well built, tall Russian replied. "They will start framing tomorrow now that the footings have all been finished. The concrete for the lower levels will be ready to pour. The biggest problem is getting all of the special manufactured stuff. You know, the bars, training equipment et cetera. We'll be using your basement temporarily until the new building is ready."

"Let me know if you have any trouble. I'm sure I can expedite it." Burnham remarked.

The men came to the bottom of the stairs and Arcady punched the code into the large, steel door. The men walked through and entered a long hallway with numerous steel doors on either side.

"They're in the common room. We still don't have all the mounts and frames in yet. They'll be here in a few days. But you wanted to get started."

"How many?" Burnham asked as the men walked down the hallway.

"Five," Arcady answered. "And I don't think you'll be disappointed."

Arcady stopped at the third door down the hall on the left. He entered a series of numbers on the keypad and the lock clicked open.

All eyes in the room turned to the door as the two men entered. Lem immediately got to his feet and screamed at

the inquisitive girls. "Eyes front! Eyes front!" He had a
long whippy stick and struck out at the first woman. She
shrieked and made to defend herself. Lem went down the
line behind the naked, kneeling girls, slapping the whip
against their flesh. The young women cried out and the
room was filled with their panicking voices.

"Silence!" Lem called out and struck the women again.
One by one, the terrorized women knelt back into place,
their eyes glued to imaginary spots on the wall ahead of
them. There was sniffling and low, pitiful whining, but the
women were otherwise still and quiet.

Arcady laughed. "As you can see, they're all fresh and
untrained. Just like you asked for."

"When did they arrive?" Burnham asked.

"This morning. They were taken from their shipping
tubes about an hour ago. They're wide awake now and
ready to begin their training."

Burnham walked slowly down the line of frightened,
kneeling women. His six foot, heavy frame towered over
them. He stopped at the third woman, one of the long
haired brunettes. He bent over and lifted her chin with his
hand. Her eyes were watering and her lips were trembling.

"Very pretty," Burnham remarked. "Nice." He continued to walk down the line until he passed the blond on
the end. Then he walked down the line again, this time
behind the kneeling women, admiring their naked backs
and their delicious curves.

"Okay," he said. "Go ahead."

Arcady nodded to Ozzie, who picked up a cardboard
carton from the floor next to him. He passed by the line of
women, dropping two pairs of leather bracelets in front of
each of them. Lem followed him dropping a leather collar
next to the bracelets.

"This batch all speak English so that will make things a
little easier," Arcady informed Burnham. English was the

'lingua franca' of Kalikastan when dealing with female slaves. There were so many from so many different places that it would have been impossible to know all of their languages. Since many of the captives had a working knowledge of English, using it during training made sense.

"Once we have some girls trained, we'll have one of them act out our orders for them, you know, like a pantomime," he added.

This 'batch' had been diverted to Burnham's estate by Khalid Rashid. Khalid was the principal importer of young women into Kalikastan. In fact, all of the shipments from the Elizabeth warehouse operated by Jake's crew were sent from Newark Airport directly to Khalid. The next shipment of young, desirable American women was not due until next week. So Khalid had sent over a batch of young, desirable British girls to Burnham instead.

Burnham was eager to break into the slave market in Kalikastan. He had become enamored of the lifestyle he had found here. He had moved his corporate operations to his estate from New York. He had purchased his own teams of ponygirls and he was determined to start his own slave training center. It wasn't that he had abandoned the effort to rescue his only and favorite niece, Maddy, it was just that once he had seen and experienced the benefits of owning the flesh of pretty young women, he decided to kill two birds with one stone. He would rescue Maddy if he could. But if not, well, he would have his little hobbies.

The oil and gas pipeline that he was constructing on contract from a joint enterprise formed by a consortium of various Western governments not only would bring in a lot of graft, which he was distributing to the various criminal 'families' in Kalikastan in exchange for Kalikastani citizenship and the sprawling estate on which his mansion sat, but would create several boom towns of construction workers. They would need whores to service them and so the market for trained and subservient sexual slaves was very bullish. Burnham wanted to seize on this market opportunity. And he wanted to be in a position to pick the best for himself.

Arcady stepped up so that he was in front of the line of young women. "You have before you two pairs of leather bracelets and a leather collar," he told them. "You will now lock one bracelet on each of your wrists and ankles. When you are finished, you will place the collar around your necks." He paused a moment. "You will start now."

The disbelieving, frightened girls took a moment to absorb the tall Russian's command. Lem jumped at them and started beating them again with the long, leather whip. "You will obey an order when it is given, you sluts!" he yelled. "Do what you're told!" He struck the girls indiscriminately as he went down the line behind them. As he passed them they began to hurriedly clasp their arms and ankles into the bracelets. When the last girl had circled her neck with the collar and locked it into place, Lem screamed at them again. "Resume positions!" he yelled striking them again.

Five new, collared, slave girls knelt on the floor, their watery eyes peering into nothingness ahead of them. Their trembling hands were atop their heads.

Arcady looked over to Burnham. "Which one would you like to start with?" he asked.

"The brunette, the third one," Burnham answered.

Lem stepped over to her and whipped her twice on the back. "Stand up!" he yelled. The girl sprung to her feet, squealing with pain.

"Come here," Arcady ordered in a low but commanding voice. The frightened girl took three steps forward. Arcady ordered her to turn around and face the other women. As she complied, Ozzie lowered a chain from the ten foot high ceiling. "Raise you arms," Arcady told the trembling girl.

When the girl saw that her hands were going to be locked over her head, she started to plead with Arcady, her wavering voice tinged with a hint of Scottish brogue. "Please don't hurt me, mister! I'll do what you say, please!" Her voice was whiny and desperate. She had bright blue eyes and thin lips. Her body was well tanned with small triangles of white over each breast. A sharp "V" of white rose from between her thighs. She had a thick, black thatch of pubic hair. Her legs were long and graceful. There was a small, brown birthmark just to the left and above of the nipple on her right breast.

Lem reacted instantly to her little speech. He swung the whippy stick viciously across her breasts. The girl let out a loud scream, "Ahhhhhhhhhhh!" and doubled over to protect herself.

"No talking!" Lem yelled at her. "Stand up!" At this last commend he laid one across her back. A long thin line of red appeared.

"Ohhhhhhhhhh!" the girl cried out. She straightened herself immediately, tears now flowing down her face. "Hands up!" Lem screamed. He was standing about a foot away from the girl's face.

The girl jerked her hands into the air above her. Ozzie was prepared and he joined her wrist bracelets together and fastened them to the chain. Crouching at the girl's feet, he connected the bracelets on her ankles. He then went over to the wall, pushed a button, and the chain rose towards the ceiling. He waited until the pretty, long haired brunette was fully extended and stopped the chain.

The other girls were sniffling and crying as they saw their companion stretched out her full length. Adele Ferguson's toes just barely touched the soft carpet beneath her. She was frantically hoping that she was in some kind of nightmare.

Fergie, as her friends called her, worked in an office in the financial district of London. She was 22 and had moved down to the big city after graduating from a small business college in Glasgow three months before. A week or two ago, she had come to the attention of a certain individual while riding the underground to her one room bedsitter in Soho. Careful note was made of her shapely form, the pretty, tanned legs beneath her miniskirt and the smooth, beauteous aspect of her facial features. She was followed to where she lived and discrete inquiries were made.

Four nights ago, Fergie thought that she heard someone in her room. She was reaching for her cell phone to call the police when a hand covered her mouth and she felt a pinprick in her arm. Dazed, she was powerless to prevent the two men who had come to claim her from tying her hands behind her back, gagging her and rolling her into a long, canvas carrying bag. An hour later, she was rolled back out of the bag, naked except for the pink and white panties she slept in. She was blindfolded and stuck in a cage. Now she was in Kalikastan, hoping that she would wake up soon and find herself back snug in her bed.

She wanted to beg and plead, but was afraid of the man with the whip. She had never been treated so, few women have. She knew that something terrible was about to happen and could not believe that there was not some way to avoid it.

When the girl saw Arcady with a four foot long, leather covered, rattan cane in his hand, she lost all hope of deliverance.

"Oooooooooooooh!" she cried as the first blow struck across the front of her thighs. She moaned again when the next blow struck her across her tight, flat tummy. When the cane's bite landed on her tender, heavy breasts, she resumed her oral effort to obtain mercy.

"Ooooooooooooooh! Please stop, please! I'll do what you want! Please, please don't hit me again! Please!"

Arcady worked the leather covered cane all over her body. She tried to twist and turn to avoid the blows, but her bound ankles frustrated her efforts. When she found that she was finally able to turn her bruised breasts away from the man wielding the cane, he began to torment her back, her pleasant rump and the back of her thighs.

While Fergie screamed and wailed her pain, begging frantically for surcease, the four other girls were crying and shaking with fear. One of the girls, Mary McCarthy, she had been on holiday from her home in Belfast when she was taken, lost control of herself and wet the soft, maroon rug. Later, after her turn with the whip, she would be made to clean up the mess she had made with her tongue.

When Arcady had delivered the last blow, he handed the whip off to Lem. The girl sagged in her chains, moaning piteously. Ozzie lowered the chain and loosened Fergie's strained wrists from it. She sank to her knees. Lem gave her a sharp blow with the cane on her ass and yelled, "Back in position!" Even in her distress, the young woman was able to comprehend this mandatory instruction and she crawled over to her spot and, turning, got up on her knees and placed her hands on her head.

Arcady turned to Burnham. "Would you like me to show you the rest of the place?"

Burnham, whose lusts had been raised by watching the naked, young Briton dance to the whip, tore his eyes away from the enticing, red striped flesh of the girl. "Of course," he answered the tall Russian.

As they were leaving the room, Lem yelled out to another of the unhappy girls, "Stand up!"

* * * * * * * * * * * * *

Jackie left Jake alone in the hotel suite at about 4 A.M. She had morning dates and needed to get back to her apartment to shower and change. She also wanted to get at least a couple hours sleep. Jake had told her to act normal and to continue her normal routines. She would be contacted when they were ready to start her journey to Kalikastan. She rode the elevator to the 20th floor and walked down the hall to her apartment. It was an expensive place to live, three blocks off of the 'Loop' and with a nice view of Lake Michigan. She unlocked the door and stepped inside. As she was walking to the bedroom, she began to disrobe, pulling her clingy, silken blouse over her head. She was just pulling it off of her arms when she felt someone step behind her. A cloth was fastened over her face and she inhaled in surprise. In a second, all went dark.

* * * * * * * * * * * * *

Jake watched from his rental as the two men carried the large trunk to their car. Another man, who had been waiting, popped the lid to the car's trunk and the traveling trunk was placed inside. The three men jumped into the car and sped off.

The men who had seized Jackie were not part of his crew. They were part of an independent operation that worked out of the South Side. Jake had placed an 'order' with them, tipping them off to Jackie's identity and address. They had only waited for a cell phone call from him to act.

In two days, days in which Jackie would sit bound, gagged and blindfolded in a steel cage, Mary Ellen, a beautiful, statuesque, blond lesbian who now ran the

Elizabeth operation for Jake, or one of her girls, would pick her up and drive her to their warehouse. A day or two after that, she would be again rendered unconscious, placed in an aluminum tube and shipped to her fate via air freight. With any luck, she would be at Burnham's estate within a week, shorn and shaved, ready to receive the tattoos that would denote her as property of Michael Burnham.

He hadn't told Jackie that she would be picked up so soon. He wanted her to act as if she had no foreknowledge of her fate. Also, he wanted to eliminate any chance that she would blab to a friend about 'not being around for a little while'. If she had said no, he would have called off the snatch. But he was pretty sure, too sure, that she would say yes. How could a street girl resist the prospect of independent wealth? He felt bad about putting such irresistible bait in front of the girl. He really liked her. Hopefully, it would all turn out for the best.

CHAPTER SIX
A PONY IS BORN

The tall, brown skinned, African-American female stood in the middle of the courtyard of Khalid's slave center. Five pretty, little, white girls knelt in a row next to her. Their mouths were busy servicing the men of Khalid's crew, a tradition at Khalid's as long as anyone could remember. It was their introduction to their new role in life, taken within the hour of their arrival in the long, silver, shipping tubes.

This was an American lot, and all the pretty girls had been taken from comfortable, middle class lives, away from boyfriends, colleges, the bar scene, rock videos, smart, stylish clothes, frat parties and other mainstays of 21st century life for the average, young, white, middle class American female. It was quite a departure from their norms to be servicing the cocks of strange men. For Jackie, it would have been rather routine, but, ironically, she was the one standing, her gag filling her mouth, with nothing to do.

It was strict policy that any female destined to be transformed into a ponygirl not be subject to sexual use until she had been delivered to her new owner. And so Jackie stood, her arms bound behind her, her legs spread, naked, part of her enjoying the distress of all those pretty, little, white girls.

There was another part of her that was terrified beyond any of her expectations. She had been startled when she was accosted in her apartment the morning that she had left Jake. At first, she failed to make the connection. But when she woke up and found that she had not been murdered, but was bound, gagged and blindfolded in a steel cage just big enough for her scrunched up, tall frame, she understood what had happened. For a while, maybe an hour or two, she was cool with it. She had been prepared for something like this. But as the time dragged on, she became apprehensive. The steel bars of her cage poked into her ample flesh. Her mouth began to ache from the fact that it was distended by the thick leather plug that had been installed there. She had to pee. And the strain in her back from being bent over was starting to be more than annoying.

She had tried to detect the presence of other persons by listening for them but then realized that her ears were stopped up, cutting off all sound. She was locked in a world all by herself, alone with her thoughts and fears.

Soon, Jackie was moaning, trying to obtain communication with someone. She wanted to explain that she was going along with the program, that it was all right, she wouldn't give any trouble, that there was no need for her to be so horribly confined. The only answer that she got was a dose of ice cold water from a hose directed by an anonymous hand. She got the message and after that she was quiet, keeping her distress to herself.

Twice, a man came by, removed her gag and gave her something to drink. The first time, she had tried to talk but was rewarded by a vicious slap to the face. The second time, although by now her fear had grown to outright terror, she kept her piece to herself.

She also learned to pee right where she knelt. There was a stream of water that passed under the cages that whisked away all liquid wastes. Once, she had been washed and cleaned and allowed to defecate in a little pan.

Jackie had no idea how long she had been held captive when she felt herself dragged from her cage. She was mounted to a post, her arms spread out to either side of her, her legs tied to rungs in the floor. After a while, she felt soft, feminine hands caressing her body, measuring her breasts, stroking her sex to moistness. The hand lingered on her pussy until she was moaning with need and then abruptly left. Her hood was pulled off and she saw the face of a tall, imperious, blond woman with a pretty but businesslike face. Jackie's gag was removed and her mouth and teeth inspected. She tried to talk again, but the woman struck her hard across her face and told her to "shut up!"

There was a long ride in some kind of truck and then another cage. It was then that she decided that she had made a mistake. This was too much to ask of anyone. She wanted out and would say so the first chance that she got. She never got the chance. Each time that her gag was removed, a bottle was shoved into her mouth filled with a tepid but refreshing liquid or a kind of mush that substituted for a meal. The third time that her gag was removed, she started to speak. The gag was unceremoniously shoved back in and she lost her opportunity for liquid or food. The next time, she stayed silent.

The remorseful, brown skinned whore was finally taken from her cage. She walked a short distance over a concrete floor. She felt a jab of a needle in her behind. Her stupefied body was laid in a long, silver canister, a mouthpiece was substituted for her gag and the container was closed. An hour later, silver tubes containing the unconscious bodies of her and six pretty, little, white girls were on their way to Kalikastan.

Now, standing in Khalid's courtyard, Jackie relished the chance to stand and stretch her cramped leg muscles. She was sure that soon there would be someone that she could talk to to get in contact with Jake and call the whole thing off. When she and the other young women were lined up in the middle of the huge cobblestone courtyard where she now stood, a cruel looking fat man dressed like a Middle Eastern potentate came out and selected one of the girls.

She was taken to a gibbet that was mounted in a slot cut out of the cobblestones, hung there by her arms and mercilessly whipped. Jackie's stomach grew tense as she watched the pretty, little, white girl dance to the lash. She heard her beg for relief, plead for mercy, offer up her body, her mouth, all of herself if only the whipping would stop. It was after the whipping that the other five naked young girls who were standing next to Jackie, their arms bound behind them and thick gags in the mouths, were ordered to their knees. Their gags were removed and men lined up to be serviced.

As far as Jackie went, all that she had to suffer was the filthy hands of the fat man caressing her breasts and the slit between her thighs. If she could have, Jackie would have spit in his face. Her face must have shown her disdain for her assailant since he laughed when he saw her enraged eyes and called several other men to come over and look at them.

Eventually the women in Jackie's 'flight' were allowed to rise from their knees and they and Jackie were led into one of the barracks type buildings. Jackie and the other girls were kept in individual open door stalls throughout the rest of the day and through the night. A collar had been affixed around her neck. Her wrists were tied behind her back with a leather thong and her collar connected to a ring in the wall by a chain. There was a little bench that she could sit on. Men came by at various intervals to gawk at the tall, big boned, brown skinned woman. They all knew that she was destined to become a ponygirl and they admired her strong form and the spirit she showed in her eyes when she stared back at them.

Twice, she and the other 30 or so naked, bound prisoners that were kept in the stone barracks were led out and forced to run around the courtyard as fast as they could, their naked breasts flailing, their bare, tender skin receiving encouragement by the whips held by the men. Jackie went with the program. In fact, she appreciated the chance to get out of her stall and do something else but sit around all day. Afterwards, she morosely allowed herself to be brought back to a stall and attached to the chain from the wall.

Dinner time was special. Her insides burned with hunger as she knelt on the floor of her stall and licked her mush-like dinner from a bowl. When she had been ungagged so that she could eat, the attendant had shown her his whip and made it crystal clear that she was to remain silent. She was so hungry that she would have agreed to anything.

When the man came back to collect her bowl, Jackie spoke to him quietly. "Please," she said, "I've got to talk to somebody. There's been a mistake. I've got to get out of here."

The man answered with a mighty crack of the whip across Jackie's pillow-like breasts. "Oooooow!" she yelled as the pain from the blow went through her. "What the fuck are you doing!" she yelled. "Fuck you, you asshole!" she yelled. "I want to speak to somebody, you hear!"

The man answered by swinging his whip and striking Jackie's exposed flesh three more times in rapid succession. "Oooooh!" she called out as she danced and writhed to avoid the blows. "Stop! Stop!"

A second man had come to her stall and he laughed and exchanged some words with the first. They weren't really supposed to beat prospective ponygirls and so they needed to take direct action against the rebellious captive. The two men jumped the tall, dark colored girl and struggled her to the floor. "Get off me you motherfuckers!" she yelled. "Fuck you! Fuck you!"

One man gained superiority over Jackie's torso while the other grabbed her legs. Her ankles were quickly tied together. That man then came to Jackie's head with her gag in his hand. She twisted and turned her head, fighting off his efforts to gag her. She had stopped cursing because she didn't want to open her mouth for fear that the man would shove the gag in. He was able to clamp his free hand over her mouth and nostrils. Jackie heaved and twisted her body to get free. She tossed her head from side to side to liberate her mouth and nose. The demand for breath began to get serious when the man who had captured her torso leaned back and gave her a solid punch to her midsection. Jackie moaned with the pain. The other man removed his hand from Jackie's mouth and she gasped for breath, her mouth yawning wide. The man stuffed her mouth with the leather plug and buckled it behind her head.

Once the gag was in place, the men dropped Jackie's body to the ground. The rebellious woman was straining to regain her breath through her nose. The men laughed and ran their hands over her soft, firm breasts and down along her taut belly. Jackie started to whine behind her gag. Why didn't the men listen to her? How could they do this? Her fire lit eyes stared at the amused men. She pulled her joined legs back and tried to kick at them. This engendered more laughter. Two other men had appeared at the door to Jackie's stall and they joined in the merriment. A tall, muscular, grey haired man appeared. He was not amused. He barked an order to the men. In a moment, Jackie's body was pulled out straight. Her ankles were affixed to a hook in the floor as was her collar. As a last touch, a black cloth bag was draped over her head and pulled tight around her neck.

For the rest of the night, Jackie lay confined to the floor in her stall. From time to time, she would issue muffled yells and screams from inside the black bag over her head and twist and turn her torso to get free. It was impossible,

of course. The former call girl was desperate. She realized
that she was in that place Jake had talked about, Katistan or
something like that. She desperately wanted to call the
whole thing off. If what she had gone through so far was
anything like what being a ponygirl would be like, she
wanted no part of it. A million bucks was not half enough.
If only she could get these assholes to understand!

Jackie eventually fell asleep. She was still bound and
blinded by the hood. In the morning, she heard the noise
of the other women shuffling out of the barracks,
apparently going for their run. Jackie wanted to go, but the
men couldn't be bothered with her. In a little while her
processing as a ponygirl would begin and it didn't make
sense to have to deal with her rebelliousness until the time
came for that.

The other captive women had been returned to their
stalls and been fed breakfast when the men finally came for
Jackie. Her body tensed when she felt the men's hands on
her. Usually, one man was enough to lead the lamb to its
slaughter since most women became docile and resigned to
their fate when confronted by the men's immeasurably
greater, ruthless power. But they weren't taking chances
with the 'chocolate girl' as they called her.

Jackie's ankles and neck were released from the floor
and her body was lifted up by two men holding her legs and
her torso. She was placed on a gurney and strapped down.
Jackie didn't know what was happening, but she knew that
it couldn't be good. She twisted and turned her body
attempting to free herself. This generated more amusement on the part of her captors as they played with her
naked breasts. She felt her gurney rolled out of the
building and across the courtyard over the large
cobblestones. The gurney went up a little ramp and back
into a building. She was brought down a hall and into a
little room.

This was the shaving room. Countless, tall, well built, big breasted, young women had been brought here and had their hair reduced to a ponytail rising out of the back of their heads. It was Jackie's turn. Two more men were waiting for Jackie and the four men prepared to mount her in the chair and secure her head for the barber. Jackie twisted and turned her body, screaming behind her gag as the men lifted her from the gurney and attempted to put her in the chair.

The problem was that her arms needed to be released from her back and affixed to the arms of the chair. But the men had handled recalcitrant young women before, maybe not as vociferously rebellious as Jackie, but difficult to handle none the less. There was a system. The men dropped Jackie into the chair. She was doubled over at the waist while two men reached behind her and unfastened her wrists. The fourth man strapped her legs to the bottom of the chair. Once Jackie's arms were freed, they were pulled in front of her. The man holding her torso pushed it back into the chair while the other two each placed an arm on the armrests. The fourth man tied the straps around each arm, fastening them in place.

The distraught young woman resisted the men with all of her might. She was strong, but not stronger than four experienced men. She was locked into the chair quickly. The hood was removed from her head and her gag undone. While the gag was being removed, a frame was set over her chest and hooked into the chair. Before she had the opportunity to speak, the men clamped an apparatus around her chin and cheeks. It had a long, leather wad attached and it was shoved into Jackie's protesting mouth. Screws were turned, a strap adjusted and the men stepped back. Jackie's head was now immobilized. She tried to jerk it free, to no avail. Now her head could be shaved.

A heavyset, blond woman entered the room with a cart. She wore a flowing, pink and white, peasant's skirt and a fluffy, white blouse. She was in her early thirties and her face was smooth, plump and shiny. She had strong, peasant's arms and large, ripe breasts that bulged her blouse out like a podium. She was smiling happily and nodded a friendly hello to the men.

On the cart was a steaming bowl of water, an electric razor, a straight razor, a shaving brush and some towels. Usually, the soon to be ponygirl was left by herself with the merry barber to experience the shaving of her head and the removal of her other hair in relative isolation, but this time two of the men stayed to watch over her.

When Jackie heard the electric razor turned on, she tried desperately to free her head. She managed to move her head slightly, but it was firmly fastened into place. As her long, brown hair fell all around her, Jackie cried and moaned. They were going to do it to her! They were making her into a ponygirl! "Please, please," she begged in her mind, "don't let them do this!"

By the time the large, blond woman had removed the long strands of Jackie's hair, aside from the skein that would constitute her ponytail, Jackie had resigned herself to the inevitable. These men were too strong for her. She had no ability to fight them. She would have to let them do what they wanted. Later, surely she would get a chance to talk to somebody. There must be some way out of this!

The two men who had remained in the room took advantage of Jackie's relative calm to untie her ankles from each other and attach her legs to two armatures by the bottom of the chair. The woman behind Jackie was singing sweetly as she scraped a layer of foamy soap from the girl's head. She had done this many times. She thought that the ponygirls were so cute. She never missed the races if she could help it. Unfortunately, she lived here in the capital,

Dlitski, and the races were held so far away. But her husband liked them too and she often was able to convince him to make the long drive to the nearest estate to watch the ponies run.

Jackie began to cry. It had been a long time since the tough street girl had cried. She was filled with self pity. How could Jake have led her into this, she thought. Why did she ever agree to it?

After she had removed the dark skinned girl's stubble, the blond woman patted her face and gave her a little kiss on her forehead. It was so hard on these women to be transformed. They clung so desperately to their humanity. But, she imagined, they soon got used to it. They looked so happy and cheerful pulling their little wagons and carts.

There was a crank on the side of the chair that caused it to lean back. The woman used it now and Jackie felt herself being tilted backwards. At the same time, the armatures to which her legs were attached started to move away from the chair, spreading Jackie's thighs apart. The woman stood between Jackie's widespread legs and began to snip away at the abundant, wiry forest of brown hair above and around her sex. Jackie's body tensed and she whined and cried as she felt the pull of the scissors. When the long hairs had all been cut away, the blond woman lathered up the stubble and began to scrape it away with the straight razor. Jackie could feel the woman's strong hands turning her labia this way and that to get every last, little follicle.

She was surprised when she felt the woman's thick finger run along the length of her brown slit and begin to tease her pleasure button at the top. The girl shifted her body in her chair and tried to close her thighs. Jackie was far from shy, but she would be dammed if she would give these bastards a show. But she couldn't close her thighs and she couldn't pull her now hairless, pretty, little cunt away from the woman's probing fingers.

The blond woman felt sorry for this poor girl. She shaved three or four prospective ponygirls a week, sometimes more. But this one had struggled so hard and was so obviously, particularly upset about her transformation that she decided she deserved a little pleasure as a consolation.

The men who had remained in the room perked up when they saw the barber stroking Jackie's pussy. Jackie heard them say something teasing to the blond woman who laughed nervously but was not deterred from bringing this pretty, chocolate woman to climax. Jackie felt her lust start to rise as the woman continued to stroke her. Her right hand was caressing the soft wet tissue between the folds of her nether lips while the other hand was rubbing Jackie's tummy and caressing her breasts. The blond woman pinched Jackie's prominent, thick nipples, which had already stiffened as a result of her arousal, making her moan.

Jackie could feel her heart beating faster, her breasts grow tighter. Her loins were burning with need. She hated the woman for forcing these lusts from her, for what she had done to her, but she did not want her gentle, experienced hands to stop.

The soon to be former hooker had never been into bondage and never let any of the johns tie her up. She had one boyfriend who had bound her hands behind her back, but that was just so that he could slap her around. That was the end of him. She had never experienced the loss of control over her own orgasm that she was feeling now. Her mind said no, no, no, but her body yearned for the woman's fingers to bring her to completion. She could feel her orgasm coming like a wave getting ready to crash upon a beach. Higher and higher the wave got until its weight pushed over itself and came crashing down. The brown colored whore let the wave wash away all of her resistance. Her pussy took control of her as it spasmed and contracted, sending hard pulses of pleasure through her. "Oooooompf! Oooooompf!" Jackie yelled into the cruel gag that filled her mouth. Her body tried to twist and turn in the chair, her thighs twitched and her eyes fluttered. The blond woman kept her going and going until she could hardly stand any more. "Ahhhhhhhhh! Ahhhhhhh!" she cried as her throbs of pleasure bordered pain. "Ahhhhhhh! Ahhhhhhhhh!"

Jackie lay in the chair weak and spent when the woman withdrew her hands from her body. She had watched the nascent ponygirl's face as she came and felt happy that she had given her such pleasure. She realized that she was the last person, together with the two male guards, who would see this lovely woman's face as she came. Soon, her face would be locked away forever and only her convulsing body and moans of pleasure would signal her orgasms.

The plump, blond woman kissed Jackie on the forehead again and tweaked her breasts. She took some lotion from her cart and spread it over the shaved portions of Jackie's loins, over her bald head and over her face. She packed up her cart. Before she left, she went up to the pretty, brown skinned girl and, stroking her head affectionately with her hands, whispered to her softly in Russian, "Goodbye, little ponygirl."

The men decided to take advantage of Jackie's post orgasm stupor to ready her to be moved to the next stage. They loosened the apparatus from over her chest and pulled out the plug from her mouth. When Jackie realized what had been done, she opened her mouth to beg them one last time to release her. But before she could speak, the leather gag she had worn when she came in was reinserted and she was silenced. The men loosed her arms from the chair and brought them behind her back, fastening them together. They freed her legs and stood her up.

They were pleased that they had been able to get the girl out of the chair without any trouble. One of the men turned to open the door so that Jackie could be brought down the hall. Jackie saw her chance. She ran her shoulder into the one man, making him stumble away from her. She then leaped up and with one foot, pushed the other man in the middle of his back, forcing him out the door and to fall to the floor. She turned and saw the first man coming toward her and lifted her other foot swiftly into his crotch. He went down with a huge groan.

Jackie sprang out the door. The man who had fallen into the hallway was getting up and she gave him a mighty kick to the head with her heel. He went down moaning. Desperately, Jackie looked both ways down the hall. Her hands were fastened behind her back and she knew that she couldn't open any doors. There was light coming into the hallway from a door about thirty yards away. Jackie took off for it as fast as she could run. She had never run with such a frantic need for speed. She was down the hallway in a flash and she turned to go through the door. Just as she was crossing its threshold, a man was entering. The speed of Jackie's movement was enough to barrel him over. Jackie stumbled past him and she was outside.

When she had been left standing in the courtyard while the pretty, little, white girls sucked cock, the street girl in her had made an inventory of possible escape routes. She had noticed the stairways to the second floor of the 'U' shaped barracks building. It was enclosed on the fourth side by a tall, stone wall. There was a veranda that led all round the courtyard on the second floor and on one side, where the veranda met the wall, there was a pile of crates that a person could climb up on and vault the wall. Jackie didn't know what was on the other side, but she would take her chances.

As she streamed up the stairs, Jackie heard a male voice calling out an alarm. Men appeared all over the courtyard. There was still no one between Jackie and the wall.

Khalid had been fucking one of the poor, pretty, little white girls that had come in yesterday. She was on her hands and knees on the floor of his private chambers on the second floor, his cock buried in her hot cunt when he heard the commotion outside. He was just about to come and the interruption pissed him off. Somebody was going to get it. He pulled his long bullwhip off of the wall and stormed from the back room, through his office and out to the veranda.

Just as Khalid opened the door, he saw the naked, brown skinned American go flying past, her hands fastened behind her, her ponytail fluttering in the air. With a scorpion-like reaction belied by his size and shape, Khalid let the bullwhip fly. Jackie was about twenty feet from the crates that would lead her to possible freedom when the long, leather leash circled around her right ankle. Her foot was pulled out from underneath her and she crashed onto the deck. She tried to get up and run again, but the slaver gave the bullwhip a yank and she was pulled back off of her feet. By this time, two of Khalid's men rushed past him and threw themselves on the frantic girl.

Jackie was screaming and crying through her gag as she struggled to escape the grasp of the two men. She had almost made it! She had been twenty feet away from freedom! Her heart was anguished and her mind enraged at the injustice of her capture. The two men pulled the wriggling girl to her feet by her arms and one gave her a piercing jab to her solar plexus. She screeched with pain and panic at the loss of air. Her struggling ceased and she hung limply in the men's hands.

Khalid was stupefied. How did this happen? What fool let this ponygirl go? He turned and saw two sheepish men approaching. "You idiots!" he yelled at them. "You must be the most incompetent sons of scrofulous camels I have ever seen! Your mothers should have drowned you! How did this happen?"

The two men began to mumble their excuses. Khalid interrupted them. "I don't want to know. You two are lower than a snake's balls. I can't whip her, so maybe I should whip you!" he yelled. He turned to look at the two men who were holding Jackie's arms. She was gradually recovering her breath. Tears were rolling down her face. "Bring her to me!" Khalid ordered. When Jackie was within reach, the slaver grabbed a hold of her pony tail at the base. He lifted it high in the air, launching Jackie to her toes, causing her to moan in pain. He dragged her over to where the crates led up to the wall. He made her stand on the topmost and look over the top. The outside of the wall dropped about fifty feet. At the bottom were large, rough edged boulders. "You see! You see!" Khalid screamed at her in English. "Where were you going, slut! Nowhere! That's where you were going!"

He pulled Jackie down off of the crate and pushed her before him holding her hair tightly. Jackie whined in pain as she abjectly proceeded in the direction that she was pointed to. The muscular, grey haired man who had cut short the amusement that the men were having with Jackie the day before appeared. He took in the aftermath of the emergency.

"Serge, please take this slut downstairs and see that she finishes her processing," Khalid said in Russian. "I want her punished when she is done. And no marks!"

"Yes, Khalid," the cruel looking man answered.

Jackie was frog marched back down the stairs and back into the building. They took her into a large room with racks of leather goods mounted everywhere. While her ponytail was held tightly over her head, a man measured her and produced a leather harness. He strapped it around her upper body and then fastened her wrists to it behind her back.

"Higher!" Serge told him, and Jackie's wrists were raised until she moaned from the pain. A thick, leather collar was put around her neck.

The man went behind the counter into the storeroom and came out holding a leather hood. When Jackie saw it, her knees went weak. The strain on her scalp made her push herself back up, but her stomach was churning. "Jake said that they would hide my face, that I would have no more face! This is it! They're going to do it to me!"

Jackie whined and moaned and squirmed as the man approached with the hood. The ponytail needed to be threaded through the hole on the top before the mask was applied. Serge took hold of the ring at the front of Jackie's collar and lifted her off of the floor. Jackie felt herself choking and tried to kick her legs to gain purchase. While she was struggling, her hair was pushed through the hole in the hood. When that was done, the attendant began to pull the hood over Jackie's face.

"Let me do it!" Serge ordered. The man shrugged and stepped back. Serge lowered the gasping woman to her feet. He shook her collar so that he could get her attention. When she was staring at him, her heart pumping wildly with fear, her blood running cold, he smiled, and with his free hand pulled the mask down over her face. He grabbed the belt at the bottom and pulled it tight around her neck. She was now a pony girl.

CHAPTER SEVEN
HOME ON THE RANGE

Jake had been back from the States for a few days. He had tried several times to see Burnham, but he was either out or too busy. He had sent a coded email to him when Jackie had started on her trail to Kalikastan, but had only gotten a one word reply, "Acknowledged."

Having nothing better to do, he hung around the estate and watched the men training the young ponygirls he had acquired for Burnham. In the spring, he had driven around half of Kalikastan with Irkut, an experienced pony trader, and examined stock for sale at various estates. The idea was that while he was going around looking at ponygirls to fill Burnham's ponygirl barn, he could look for Maddy. It sounded like an impossible task, there being dozens of ponygirl estates and hundreds of ponygirls, but they knew that Maddy was what was called a yearling. The ages of ponygirls was calculated from their date of transformation from free and independent women to servile animals. First year ponies were called yearlings. So he concentrated on looking at yearlings, and a few older ponies as well so as not to raise suspicions, and had made about fifteen purchases for Burnham. He had found Maddy at one of his last stops.

He was at one of the estates and had been invited to stick around for the races. It was traditional to display the ponygirls the night before they raced and have a big party to mark the occasion. Jake had a hunch that Maddy would be there that night and he was right. He found her, her collar attached to a pole, displayed naked and with her legs fastened apart for the amusement of the guests. The thing that made finding Maddy especially difficult was that all of the ponies wore tight, clingy hoods that covered all of their identifiable facial features. They were all selected because they matched a certain body type and so they all looked very similar. He did know that Maddy was a brunette, so he had concentrated at looking at the ponies with brown ponytails. He had one edge. He had obtained a photograph of Maddy during the investigation of her kidnapping. It showed her laughing face, but more importantly, she was wearing a bikini and it showed a small mole on her left hip. When Jake saw the mole, he knew that he had found Maddy.

He had notified Burnham and watched Maddy run the next day. She blew her competition away. She was pulling what was known as a sulky cart, a one pony cart that was typically driven by the smallest man that could be found, often a midget or a dwarf. There were two sulky races, the 1500 meter and the 3000. Maddy ran the 1500, unusual for a yearling. She had started the season as part of two pony yearling team, but had gotten so good that when one of Grobgy's sulkies went down with an injury, she was moved up to take her place. Based on a combination of hers and her predecessor's records, she qualified for the championship tournament.

Jake and Burnham had attended the tournament and had watched Maddy run several heats. She was considered a long shot, but had clawed her way to the finals. In the final she had beaten the overall favorite, an Andalusian pony named Isabella. Burnham had wrangled an invitation to Grobgy's celebration party at his estate. Burnham was becoming a big time player in Kalikastan, and Burnham had tried to buy Maddy, now called Lightning, from Grobgy. Grobgy had demurred and that's when the plot to challenge Grobgy to a stakes race was hatched. Jake was sent to the States to find a suitable candidate that could be trained to race Maddy. He found Jackie.

When Jake had come back from the States, the first thing that he did was look for his own personal body slave, Klara, a young, big bosomed, Dutch girl who had been a present to him from one of the estate owners. He had come to care for the enslaved, Dutch girl and, he believed, she had become enamored of him. Of course when you hold the power of life and death over someone, it's difficult to tell whether they're being obsequious or loving. But if it was just the fawning of a servile minion, it was a pretty good act.

Klara had gone through the intense training that all the slave girls suffered, and she had become a sexual plaything well before Jake met her. She had long, thick, blond hair that she often wore in a braid down her back. She was tall and svelte with beautiful curves. Her name was tattooed in Cyrillic letters across her chest and she wore the mark of the house that trained her, a fierce yellow dragon, on her lower belly. Like all the slave girls, she went naked.

Jake had stashed Klara with his boys, Martinez, Curley, Leon and Tucker, while he was away. He had put Tucker in special charge, a 6'5" giant with hands as big as frying pans and a ton of bricks demeanor. You know, the kind that you don't want to fall on you. He was fiercely loyal to Jake and, if he was good at one thing besides crushing heads, he followed orders. Jake had told him to keep Klara in the guesthouse that he and the boys had been using as a dorm and headquarters and to never leave her alone there without another of the crew present.

Since Burnham had taken over the estate, which formerly belonged to a bad guy who took a wrong turn and paid the price, Jake and his team had been kind of a security force. But they were being edged out by a local security outfit that Burnham had hired run by a hard looking bastard named Nicolai Boradin. Jake didn't trust him and had warned Burnham not to put himself too much in Boradin's thrall. Burnham had told him not to worry.

Klara was ecstatic when she saw that Jake had returned. It was the first time that he had seen her really smile. The naked slave girl had been pouring glasses of ale for Martinez and Curley who were sitting at the well worn, dark oak table in the comfortable, peasant style kitchen when Jake walked in. She dropped the pitcher right in the middle of the table and ran to him. Amber colored ale spread all over the table and Martinez and Curly jumped up with a howl. Beaming ear to ear, Klara fell at Jake's feet and placed her forehead on the floor, her hands behind her back.

"Master," she said in her Germanic accent, "I serve you!"

The pretty, young, blond slave girl didn't have too much English, and four words strung together were about the most that Jake had ever heard her say. Usually, she spoke to him with her soft, voluptuous lips, her expert hands and the tantalizing crevasse between her thighs.

"Up, up," Jake urged her. He reached down, grabbed her arms and pulled her to her feet. The smile had still not left her face. He put his hands on either side of her face and kissed her lips. "Lovely Klara," he said.

Klara's body softened and she opened her lips to accept his tongue. Her hands reached out and rested lightly on his hips. A wave of desire swept through Jake as his tongue danced with hers. He felt her firm breasts press against him.

After a few moments, Jake broke the kiss. Martinez and Curly were still standing, their pants soaked in front by the spilled brew.

"It looks like you guys wet your pants," Jake said, laughing. The two men smiled wryly. Klara turned and looked and gave a gasp. She broke from Jake and seized a kitchen towel which she proceeded to frantically rub over Martinez's and Curley's crotches.

Martinez grabbed her hands and stopped her. "Jeeeze, honey," he said, "a few more rubs and I'll come in my pants." He was laughing.

There were two more pretty, naked slave girls in the room and they had run up to the table with towels to soak up the spilled beverage. Curley quickly stole away from the table his pint glass filled with the auburn elixir and a two inch frothy head. He lifted it to Jake and said, "Welcome home!"

It was a 'welcome home' indeed. Jake had been working and living with his men on this job steadily for about five months. He and his men had settled well into the customs and practices of this anarchic country, as exemplared by the two pretty, young women, attired only in their black leather collars and bracelets, their pleasantly naked breasts swaying and jiggling as they strived to eliminate the discomfort and inconvenience to their masters of the spilt beer.

It was the longest job that he had ever done, but Burnham kept paying the bills. But there was less and less for his men to do except take advantage of the growing army of slave girls that Burnham was accumulating, drink the hearty, local golden ale and await instructions.

And then there was Klara. When he ordered her to accompany him upstairs, she practically dragged him by the hand up to the second floor bedroom. She waited anxiously on the large, four poster bed, kneeling with her knees spread and her hands dutifully behind her back as he undressed. She had drawn down the bedclothes and Jake was met by the cool, smooth sheets when he lay down.

The slave girl had undone her long, golden hued, blond hair which had been fastened in a thick braid behind her back. When Jake invited her to lie down with him, she spread her voluptuous body across his, her hair spreading in a corolla around them.

Klara needed no instruction to commence the pleasuring of Jake's body. She placed her broad, wet lips on his chest and began to kiss his skin fervently. Her delicate and experienced hands caressed Jake's sides and hips.

Jake luxuriated in the slave girl's caresses. His cock had begun to stir and the heat of Klara's lips soothed and relaxed him. He had missed his slave. Jake was a stranger to love and did not know whether his feelings for the young, Dutch girl rose to that label. But he cared for her and actually had yearned for her while he was away. And he had worried about her.

While she appeared devoted to him, she was still a slave girl and wore the black leather bracelets and collar that denoted her status. Across her chest was emblazoned her slave name in Cyrillic letters and she wore on her belly the tattoo of the crest of the slave house that had broken her from a free, independent, 21st century, European woman to a throwback to ancient Roman times. Anyone could use her. Burnham had taken her and used her at his whim for four days when Jake had first arrived with her at the estate, not unlike a medieval lord taking his due from the slave girl of a minion.

Also, since in the mindset of the men who peopled this strange country slave girls were not credited with personality or individuality, it might occur to one or another of the men at Burnham's estate, or to Burnham himself, to send her off somewhere, to sell her or give her away. After all, she could always be replaced by an equally obsequious, pliant, voluptuous, young woman. In a land where the goal seemed to be to fuck as many different beautiful, young women as you could, most men would think that they were doing Jake a favor. He owned a beautiful slave girl.   But it shouldn't really matter which one. And why wouldn't he want a new one every week?

Klara's lips had descended down from Jake's chest to his belly, and her hands were rubbing his strong, muscled thighs. Her hair felt like silk as it drew across his body. He was rampant now, and the slave girl's large breasts had captured his cock between them. She slid down further and captured its head with her plump lips.

Jake groaned as he felt the heat of Klara's exciting mouth encompass the bulbous end of his fleshy tube. She circled her tongue around the sensitive skin underneath and tickled the tiny slit in its middle. Her right hand grasped the stem of Jake's joint firmly while the other caressed gently the wrinkled sac beneath. Jake's erection had made the sac tighten and drawn his testes close to his body. Klara carefully and tenderly massaged the pliant stones while her lips drew a moan of pleasure from her master.

The slave girl spread her saliva down the length of Jake's rigid manhood and then, drawing herself up closer to him, slid his pole between her pillowy breasts. She pressed them together with her hands, giving the tool a soft, moist, warm bed. Slowly, she began to move her breasts up and down, massaging Jake's prick and sending waves of pleasure through him. On each downward stroke, she captured the plump helmet of Jake's cock, sliding her hot lips across it and teasing it with her tongue.

The manipulation of his cock soon had Jake lost deep in a foggy realm of pleasurable sensation. He moaned as the pretty, ardent girl drew him closer and closer to completion. His legs were spread wide and his hips thrust back at the soft envelopment of his rod. When Klara paused her motion, the head of Jake's cock in her hot mouth, her tongue spreading its caresses around it, Jake's back arched and his hands found the head of the creature that was so wonderfully tormenting him and caressed it appreciatively. When Klara's motion began again, Jake groaned. His blood was running hot and he could feel his fluids gathering in his loins for their expulsion. All at once, his cock began to throb and pulse, jettisoning his thick, white fluid. The white spewm provided heated lubricant for his cock's journey up and down between Klara's firm yet soft breasts. Each time the head arose above the tops of the billowing orbs, Klara sucked it into her mouth, consuming greedily his viscous discharge.

Later, after showering and treating his slave girl to some oral delight of her own, Jake came back downstairs. Martinez had apparently paired off with one of the other pretty young women and Curley was still in the kitchen. He had the short haired, brunette slave on his lap and had one hand between her legs. He was watching her face intently as he stroked her moist, hairless cunt. The girl's eyelids were half closed and she was breathing heavily through her parted, swollen lips. One hand was around Curley's shoulder and the other was caressing a breast. Curley looked up when Jake came in.

"Where's Tucker?" Jake asked. He had just gotten off a half hour or so ago, but the tableau of the passionate slave girl making herself open for Curley's caresses made his manhood stir. He would have to try her out later.

Curley looked away from the passionate face of the girl. "Oh, he's probably over by the auxiliary pony barn," the heavyset, short haired blond man answered. Curly looked something like his Three Stooges namesake except that instead of being bald, he maintained a miniscule layer of blond hair around his skull. "He's taken on a project for Mr. Burnham."

"A project?" Jake asked.

"Yeah," Curley replied. "He saw Mr. Burnham out with his work ponies, you know, the two big, blond ones he got a few weeks ago, and he took a shine to them.

Burnham told him he could take care of them and give them their daily workouts. When Burnham's not around, he lets him take them for a ride in the afternoons." It was about two o'clock.

Jake knew that Curley was referring to Dora and Flora, two seven year old ponies Burnham had picked up at the second hand market held during the spring ponygirl tournament. They were tall and strong, having been part of a nine pony team pulling a heavy landau carriage for many years. They were past racing form but were still good for general usage. Burnham liked to take them for an afternoon run when he could. But all the ponies needed daily attention, exercise, feeding, cleaning. Yes, and fucking.

Ponygirls had no part in deciding how, when and by whom they were used, of course. Their sexual subjugation was both a means of reinforcing their subservient status and, also, a reward system. A ponygirl who did not receive regular use often became distracted and morose. Even though they had no way of expressing emotion through their hidden faces, their body language could speak loudly. Sagging shoulders, a bowed head, a sluggish step, all bespoke a ponygirl out of sorts. And while a spell with a whip could be a great motivator, the better practice was to provide them with regular sessions with a cock or two every day. This way they always had something to look forward to. It was a system that put a heavy demand on the trainers and grooms, and so the other male employees of the estate, the gardeners, the chauffeurs, the security men, the hangers on, and there were plenty of them, all lent a hand. It always seemed to work out.

Jake wanted to check in with Tucker since he was the chief muscle of his team. He wanted a report on the current security situation and to remind him to stay awake and careful.

When Jake reached the auxiliary pony barn, he saw the team of pale, white, long blond tailed ponies trotting steadily up the main driveway. Their large, meaty breasts were dancing nicely on their chests and their knees rose high at each step in perfect unison. Tucker was seated on the bench of the small carriage, more like a dray wagon. When the team came up even with Jake, he guided them to a halt with the reins. Ponygirls were all trained to strictly obey the signals sent to them through the reins and not to anticipate commands. If Tucker had not given a slight, but steady, pull back on the reins, the milk white ponies would have kept running until they dropped from exhaustion.

"Hiya, Jake!" Tucker exclaimed. He was grinning from ear to ear.

"Enjoying yourself, Tucker?" Jake asked wryly.

"Oh, yeah, Jake, yeah," Tucker answered. Tucker was not a Rhodes Scholar, and his communicative skills were limited. But he was built like a brick shithouse. "Did ya see Klara? I had Martinez watchin' her. She's okay, right?"

"She's fine, Tuck," Jake answered. He looked over the panting, sweating ponies. "Got yourself a little side line, here, huh?"

"Mr. Burnham said I could take care of them," Tucker said by way of answer. He jumped down off of the cart and stepped up to the two naked ponygirls. They were strapped into leather harnesses that allowed long poles to be affixed to both hips. One pole ran along the outside hip of each pony and another ran between them. The poles attached to the cart and allowed the ponies to use the strength of their legs and hips in pulling the cart. Leads ran tight from the leather harnesses back to the cart so that the ponies' backs and shoulders took their part of the load. The reins were affixed directly to the bits in the ponies' mouths for purposes of control. Even when the cart was stationary, the reins were usually pulled tight to

circumscribe the ability of the ponies to turn their heads
from side to side. Although they could see very little
through the narrow holes in the pony hoods, there was no
need for them to see anything else but straight ahead of
them. Their arms were locked behind their backs and little
mittens covered their hands to prevent any fingers getting
caught up in the traces.

Burnham had chosen black and gold as his colors and
his pony training hoods were all black as opposed to the
racing hoods which were both colors and had long black
and gold feathers running from the tops. The work hoods
were plain black. They fit tightly over the ponies' heads
and erased all individuality from their faces. The hoods
had a wide oval opening for the ponies' mouths which were
almost always, except when put to specific use, kept filled
with a thick leather gag or a hard, leather covered, steel bit
that rode up high towards the back of their mouths,
stretching the corners of their lips back into a strange
grimace. A steel plate lay down across the tongue and
pressed down painfully on it when the reins were pulled
back. A good driver could bring a team to a halt with just
modest pressure, but not all drivers were good and
sometimes a driver just wanted to enforce a little discipline
or emphasize reaction time during training.

Dora and Flora's bits were deep in their mouths and
their black encased heads looked forwards dutifully.
Tucker came around and petted their gleaming, sweat
covered breasts while mumbling something soothingly to
them. Jake watched as Tucker reached into his pocket and
produced two little pieces of soft candy which he slipped
into their mouths under their bits. When he stood back,
Jake could hear the ponies slurping on them noisily.

"I need to talk with you, Tuck," Jake told the man who
was watching his charges masticate admiringly. "We need
to keep our eyes and ears open. Burnham's hired this

security team and I need to make sure that they're on the up and up."

Tucker, as if he just realized that Jake was talking to him, looked over. "Sure, Jake," he sad. "I watch out all the time. There's about fifteen of them. They come and go in the black Mercedes all day. From what I've seen of them they look like they know how to handle the Uzi's they carry pretty well. There's usually four on guard at the house, two at the gate and four patrolling. I seen them out with ponygirl teams. Around dinner, they mostly all congregate around the bunk house and afterwards go up to the pony barn for a fuck or two. If I was going to hit the place, I'd do it around 8 o'clock in the evening. Nobody would notice much a couple of extra cars pulling up and you could get almost all of them at one fell swoop in the barn. You might have to take out a few of the ponies and the other staff, but you'd get all but a couple of the security guys."

Jake was taken aback by Tucker's comprehensive report. Sometimes the guy amazed him.

"Uh, okay," he said. "Keep yourself armed. Okay?"

"Check, Jake," the big man replied.

Jake could see that he was more taken up with the dismantling of the apparatus that held the two ponygirls in their stocks. He unclipped the poles from their hips and unstrapped the harnesses from around their torsos, cooing and sweet talking them the whole time. He turned to Jake. "I'm gonna take them in the barn now and give them a rubdown. You want to fuck one of them?"

"No thanks," Jake replied. "Not today."

"Well, let me know if you do," Tucker suggested. "Dora's got a real fine mouth, she's very patient and gives a long, gentle suck." He took the right nipple of the pony that Jake assumed was Dora and gave it a little pinch. The pony shuddered slightly. "Flora likes to fuck," he said now teasing the nipple of the other pony. "She seems to really like it when you dump your load in her rear. Her whole body shakes."

"I'll keep that in mind," Jake said.

While Jake turned to go up to the main house, Tucker took the rings in the two ponies' noses by a finger of each hand and gently led them across the stone pathway and into the auxiliary pony barn. It was much like the main barn, but smaller. There was a rub down table in the common area and Tucker parked the pony called Dora next to a thick post, tying off her nose ring to a hook, and placed Flora's body up against the table. The table was mounted on a hinge so that it could be tilted up. All Tucker had to do was lean Flora against it, secure her collar and ankle bracelets to hooks in the table and push her forwards. When she was face down on the table, her legs spread, he unlocked her arms and refastened her wrists at the top corners.

Tucker loved to handle the former human female's flesh. It was smooth and soft, yet hard. His strong hands dug deep into the back and shoulder muscles of the pony until it moaned with painful pleasure. There was a sponge with warm soapy water and he washed the sweat off of the supine creature. He poured a liniment ointment on its leg muscles and thighs. When he was done, he refastened the pony's hands behind its back and then flipped it over so that he could address the front. He was especially attentive to the generous breasts, massaging them until the pony moaned and squirmed beneath his hands. He could just see the pupils of its eyes darting back and forth inside the small eyelets. It was funny, he thought, he was getting to know these two ponies so well but had never seen their faces. One of the grooms handled their morning ablutions. It was just as well. He liked them just as they were and the thought of watching them go from pony to almost human to pony again didn't appeal to him.

Tucker massaged Flora's sex until it was loose and moist. Then he removed her from the table and let Dora have her turn. Dora was more of a moaner than Flora and she noisily expressed her pleasure as Tucker spread his large, powerful hands all over her body. The ponies both still wore their bits, which allowed more sound to escape their mouths than did the all encompassing, leather shields and plugs. Dora's voice seemed more high pitched than Flora's, but her sounds were no more recognizable as words. Tucker had not taken the time to wonder what language they had spoken back when they were women. He was not a deep thinker. He spent most of his time in the moment and hadn't the inclination for speculation or conjecture. To him things were as they were and that was that. Dora and Flora were ponygirls and, as far as he was concerned, always had been.

When he had Dora squirming and moaning, his hand buried in her quim, he released her from the table. He wasn't teasing them, but was just warming them up. It was a routine and he knew that the ponies had come to anticipate it.

When he released Dora from the table, he had affixed the back of her collar to a chain that ran down from a beam and fastened her ankles to rings in the floor so that she was standing with her legs spread wide apart. He now brought Flora over to her and removed her steel bit. Flora was breathing hard and licked her lips in anticipation. Grabbing Flora's back collar ring, Tucker bent her head over until her mouth was level with Dora's breast. He guided her head forward and the pale white ponygirl's lips encircled the large, stiff nipple, tight with building lust.

The ponygirl's mouth worked Dora's breast and nipple ardently. She dragged her rough, broad tongue across the areola and bit the nipple delicately with the edges of her teeth. Dora moaned and made a whinnying sound as the pleasure of Flora's mouth was forced upon her. Tucker guided Flora's black clad head to the other nipple and let her devote her lustful attentions there for a little while. He could tell that these two ponies had a lot of affection for each other. He had seen the other ponies caress each other for the visual pleasure of their masters, and they never had quite the same amount of passion or devotion to their tasks. Dora and Flora hungered for each other's flesh.

Having permitted Flora to supp at Dora's fat, ripe breasts, he pulled her head back from Dora's teat and guided the pony to her knees. Flora certainly knew what was coming, but she was patient and docile, even though her breath was coming hard and fast. It was only when Tucker eased her face between Dora's extended legs that her tongue darted from her mouth and found the already moistened crevasse between them.

Tucker stood back and let Flora do her work. She was an orally fixated pony and Dora was the recipient of the benefit today of that not uncommon trait. When your mouth was imprisoned and/or confined harshly almost 24 hours a day, the opportunity to use it was almost always welcome. And using it well meant that the opportunity would come more often. The salty taste of a hardened cock, the pungent flavor of an excited pussy would seem like ambrosia after the daylong diet of saliva laced leather.

Tucker pulled out a smoke and watched as Dora's hips ground back into the mouth that had buried itself into her cunt. Flora's head was tilted up, giving her a dramatic, close, bird's eye view of the sharp taloned, black and red falcon burned into Dora's tight, flat belly, the icon of her training estate. Flora's tattoo was the same, meaning that they had probably been together for most of their seven years as ponygirls.

Flora's tongue darted out and teased the nub of flesh at the apex of Dora's sex. Dora's knees seemed to go week and her body sagged as she groaned with pleasure, her voice a high alto. Her large breasts, their ends still wet from Flora's lips, trembled and shook as the ponygirl reacted to Flora's tormenting tongue. When Flora seized her sister pony's clit between her lips, Dora's body began to shake and quiver. She called out as she came, "Gaaaaaaaaaa! Gaaaaaaaaa!" her outcry distorted by the hard bit jammed tightly across the inside of her mouth. Her black hooded head waived back and forth as she pushed up and down with her knees. Flora slowed her oral caresses as Dora's body began to recover from the throes of her orgasm. She was kneeling back on her haunches, her black covered head tilted upwards, her bound hands unconsciously clenched as she breathed in the aroma of the standing pony's orgasmic discharge. Dora's chest was heaving, her skin mottled red across her chest, offsetting the somewhat faded blue of her tattooed name that lay there. When Flora began her oral caress again, Dora gave a mighty groan and her body shook and quaked.

Tucker let the ponies work through a couple of orgasms before he gently pulled Flora's head back by her long, thick, blond ponytail. He reinserted the cruel bit and locked it behind her head. There was a small sawhorse nearby made especially to fit Tucker's current purpose and he pushed the pony's hips against it. It had wide legs and a leather padded top. Tucker fixed Flora's ankles to the legs and, using a thin, metal chain, connected her nose ring to a ring on the base on the other side. He pulled her head down until she was bent over and positioned properly.

Watching the ponygirl gemauch her partner had made Tucker's thick cock hard with purpose. He used his heavy, scarred hands to caress the golden globes of Flora's rear appreciatively. Flora's body quivered as it anticipated its use. Tucker had removed his hard crank from his pants and teased the outline of Flora's dripping slit with its head.

He was only seeking her moisture, not to delve himself into her hot canal. His mind was focused on her smaller entrance, the little brown rosette between her pale white cheeks.

With her pussy juice to ease his passage, Tucker let his steel hard cock press slowly past the tight ring of flesh that surrounded the entrance to Flora's bowels. He felt the anal tissue grip his cock tightly as he pushed on into the deep, moist warmth of Flora's ass. She groaned with pleasure as he began to saw his tool over her tender circle of flesh. All the ponygirls were trained to relish the use of their rear portals and Flora was no exception. Careful not to strain the pull of the chain attached to the ring in her nose, the big, muscular ponygirl began to push back lustfully at the cock that invaded her. When Tucker pushed forward, sinking himself deep into her, the ponygirl relaxed the tension on her rear ring to ease his passage. When he withdrew, ever so slowly, she tightened the muscle as if to make permanent his residence there.

Flora was given over to high pitched, staccato cries as her pussy throbbed and contracted in orgasm. Tucker could feel the movement of her vaginal muscles from inside her bowel and the sensation pushed him past his point of control. "Arrrgh!" he yelled as he began to pound his hips against the imprisoned rear before him. "Arrrrgh! Arrrrrgh!" he groaned loudly as his cock pumped his semen deep within. As he felt his last, almost agonizing pulse of pleasure, he grabbed the pony's flanks and pressed his belly hard against her haunches. She was whimpering with spent pleasure as he let himself soften within her.

* * * * * * * * * * * * *

It was a few days later when Jake finally was able to see Burnham. He had been away at some planning meetings for the new pipeline and he brought back with him, in tow, a sallow skinned, tall, thin, slave girl with long and narrow cat like eyes and jet black hair. She had not yet been marked and Jake could see the nervous fear in her face as Burnham led her from the back of his limousine to the house. Her hands were bound behind her and she was naked. Her eyes suggested an Asian heritage. A shield gag covered her mouth and lower face.

Burnham let Jake follow him into the house. He dragged the girl along behind with a leash. While she lacked the tattoos of a slave girl, she was already accoutered with the collar and bracelets which denoted her new status. They went up to Burnham's office on the second floor.

"You like her?" Burnham asked Jake when they entered the large, white oak paneled room. Burnham had a large, leather covered, wooden desk to match the walls, with a large, black, leather chair behind it.

"She's pretty, Mr. Burnham, but we need to talk."

"I was in Paris yesterday, meeting with some of the governmental representatives for the pipeline consortium. She was our waitress."

"She was what?" Jake asked.

"Our waitress. I think that she's part Vietnamese."

Jake was somewhat stunned. "You mean you had her snatched from the restaurant?" he asked incredulously.

"No, of course not," Burnham answered. "I had her followed and they took her from her apartment. There was something about her eyes that I liked. And I don't have a Vietnamese yet."

A blond haired slave girl scurried into the room with a tray on which sat a cloudy bottle of gin, some tonic, limes, glasses and a small bucket of ice. She set it down on a side table and fell to her knees, her forehead to the floor, her hands behind her.

"Mr. Burnham, I don't think that...." Jake began to say.

"Don't think, Jake," Burnham interrupted. "Did you fuck your little slave girl today?"

Jake hesitated. He had, of course. And he had fucked one of the other ones too. He bit his tongue.

The young, black haired, Eurasian girl stood by the desk, her leash still in Burnham's hand, her eyes spread as wide as saucers. Tears were welling up inside them. She looked over at Jake pleadingly. She still wore a heavy, black thatch between her legs and the sight of it somehow made her seem more naked. She had bright red polish on her toenails.

It had been at least two weeks since Jake had been in Burnham's office and he noticed that three small steel cages had been added to the decor. Burnham reached down and flicked one open. He looked at the girl, yanking her leash hard so that she would attend to him.

"Get in the cage, cunt," he told her.

The girl gave out a whine as she saw the small space that she was about to be condemned to. Burnham yanked the leash again. She looked back at him, terror in her eyes. With a miserable moan, she lowered herself to her knees and crawled in. Burnham removed the leash and slammed the cage door shut.

"Okay," he said, turning to Jake, "when's the new ponygirl arriving?"

"Tomorrow morning," Jake answered. His eyes were still on the lithe form of the frightened, black haired girl as she tried to maneuver her body to fit the confines of the small cage.

"Good. I've asked Irkut to take over her training. She's got to start right away," Burnham said as he picked up the telephone. He dialed three numbers and a rough, male voice answered.

"I've got a new girl up here in my office. Send someone up for her....O, yeah, that's good news.....No, I want to see her first. Bring her up."

Burnham looked up at Jake as he hung up the phone. He sat in his big, black, leather chair and motioned for Jake to take a seat in a cloth covered, padded chair to the front right of the desk. "We're all outfitted down in the basement for the training facilities."

"That's something I wanted to talk to you about, Mr. Burnham. You want me to watch your back, but they wouldn't let me down there. How can I protect you when...."

Burnham interrupted him again. "You don't need to go down there, Jake. It's not anything that you'd want to see. Just enjoy the results. I don't think you want to watch pretty, little girls being broken into obedient little sluts."

"It's not that, Mr. Burnham. It's the principle. How can I protect you when I don't know what's going on?"

There was a knocking at the door to the office. "Come in," Burnham boomed.

The door opened and a handsome, shapely woman, about forty years old with shoulder length, wavy, brown hair walked in cautiously. She was dressed in a business suit. Behind her, on either side, were two of Borodin's henchmen.

Jake thought that he recognized the woman. She wore high, light brown high heels and a tight, tan skirt that reached to just above her knees. She had on a plain, white blouse under a short, light jacket that matched her skirt. There was a pretty, brown and white cameo pin on her lapel with the outline of a cat.

The woman looked both shocked and relieved to see Burnham. She walked hesitatingly up to his large aircraft carrier sized desk. The millionaire sat back in his black, tall backed chair, a look of satisfaction on his face. The two men stood on either side of the woman, slightly behind her, menacingly.

"Oh, Mr. Burnham, I'm so happy to see you," the woman said in a nervous voice. "I got here a couple of hours ago and these men…." Her voice trailed off. She had noticed the pretty, naked, blond haired girl still crouched obsequiously at the side of Burnham's desk, her hands resting on her bare, arched back, her nose to the floor. The woman's eyes then shifted to the gagged and crying, black haired girl in the cage. She looked up at Burnham.

"Mr. Burnham, I, I…" she was searching for words to express her consternation.

It was then that Jake recognized her. It was Elizabeth Crawly, Burnham's New York secretary. Everybody called her Liz. "Now what the fuck is she doing here?" Jake thought.

"Good to see you, Liz," Burnham said, smiling. He had poured himself a glass of tonic over two fingers of gin and ice. He took a soothing sip from it.

"I, I, I'm not sure what's going on, Mr. Burnham,…" the woman started to say. She had a clear, intelligent voice. Her blue eyes were stuck at wonder.

"I'm happy that you're here, Liz. I really need you."

"But what's this all about, Mr. Burnham?" the woman asked nervously. "I mean, these girls, the cage? What's going on?"

"It's a whole new world, Liz, and you're going to be an important part of it."

"Me?" the woman asked incredulously. "I don't think that I can….'

"Shut up, Liz," Burnham interrupted, leaning forwards, his voice hard edged and angry. "Don't talk, don't speak. Just listen! You and I have a serious problem we need to work out. You've been my secretary for about seven years, Liz and you've seen a whole lot of stuff go down. Now I've paid you pretty good and you've always been discrete, but I just couldn't help but worry about what you might decide to do someday with all the dirt that you've accumulated on me."

"Dirt?' Liz exclaimed. "I haven't been accumulating any dirt on you, Mr. Burnham!" she insisted indignantly. "I'm your confidential secretary. I wouldn't...."

"Shut up, Liz!" Burnham yelled. "Shut the fuck up!"

The woman cringed at Burnham's outburst. Jake could see that two and two were beginning to make four for the frightened woman. Her tanned face had gone pale. Her lower lip was trembling mildly. She was struggling to maintain her composure. She was carrying a two gallon sized, dark brown pocketbook on her arm. She let the handle slide down to her joined hands and fidgeted with it nervously.

"Good," Burnham said, more calmly. "That's much better." He took another sip of his cool drink. Beads of moisture had formed on the glass and it left a little ring on the desk. He put it back down on a coaster. "Now as I was saying," he continued, "I always wondered what I would ever do with you. I couldn't have someone who knew about all the under the table deals, the stock manipulations, the insider trading, to just get up and walk away. Did you really think that that could happen?"

Liz started to stutter an answer, but Burnham waived her off. "A rhetorical question, Liz. You don't need to answer. I want you to know that my people found the files that you've been keeping back at your apartment. Very naughty of you, Liz. Now what was all that for?"

The sophisticated, well dressed woman's mouth hung open. Her lips were painted a mild, reddish brown. They were thin, but looked right on her pert, business-like, but pretty face. She was wearing small diamond post earrings in each ear. Just the right touch. Her hips were just a tad wide, but she carried it well and her legs were finely shaped, her thighs thin. Jake saw a small bead of sweat forming on her right temple.

"I was just keeping them to protect myself, Mr. Burnham. I wasn't going to use them against you. But I needed to know that I wouldn't get hung out to dry by you some day."

"Just right, Liz," Burnham replied. "And if the SEC or the FBI ever came asking nasty questions, well, you would have some bargaining chips, I suppose."

Liz looked back nervously at the men on either side of her, then at the two naked young women in the room and then back at Burnham. "You've got to believe me, Mr. Burnham, I would never have….."

"Shut the fuck up, Liz!" Burnham yelled again. "I play the odds, Liz. And the smart money says that I've got to shut you up. For good."

Liz's composure began to fail her. "Oh, please, Mr. Burnham, please don't to anything to me. I'll get you the documents back, all the materials, please! I'll go away, I'll never say anything! I promise!"

Burnham looked at the trembling woman with disgust. He turned and walked around the large desk until he was in front of her. She tried to step away from him, but the two mean looking men that she had come in with took hold of her arms. The one on her right removed her pocketbook from her hands and threw it on a nearby chair. Burnham's right hand leapt out and he slapped her across the face. The 'crack' of his palm playing harshly across the woman's cheek echoed through the room.

"Ohhhhhhh!" she cried out, struggling in the grasp of Boradin's henchmen. "Oh, god, please don't! Please!"

Burnham went back to his desk and pulled a pistol from a drawer. It was a silver, ivory handled, Colt .45 automatic. He returned to the shaking, now somewhat disheveled woman. He put the gun to her head. "Please get on your knees, Liz," he said, politely, but sternly. Sobbing, and with the assistance of the two men who had come in with her, Liz sank to the rug.

"You brought me all the way here to murder me?" she cried out. "Oh, god, please don't, please!"

The woman's face was a mask of fright. Jake stood. Was he going to let Burnham blow this woman's brains out right in front of him? He was stunned by the transformation he was seeing in Burnham. He knew that he was a cold, calculating son of a bitch, but murder? By his own hand? And of someone he had worked with almost every day for seven years?

Liz was blubbering. She had collapsed into a little ball on the floor. A large, circular, cream colored, woven rug lay on the polished hardwood floor in front of Burnham's massive desk. Liz's tan outfit melded with the floor covering. She was crouched tight, her hands over her head, her suit jacket stretched across her back, her stockinged legs underneath her. "Oh, please don't do this, Mr. Burnham, please, please!" she cried out desperately. "I'm sorry! I'm sorry! Please don't!"

Burnham nuzzled the large, silvery pistol against the back of Liz's head. Her whole body quivered in dreadful anticipation. Her voice went still; her arms were tightly crossed over the back of her head, crushing her thick, wavy, brown hair under them. There was a moment of deathly quiet, the only sound, Liz's low, sniveling moan. Burnham leaned over so that his face was about a foot away from Liz's ear. "You want to live, Liz?" he asked her, his voice hard edged and deliberate. "If you want to live, get back up on your knees. Do you hear me?"

Liz hesitated briefly, taking in what she had hoped that she had heard. She rose slowly from the floor to her knees. She held her trembling hands in front of her, as if in prayer.

Her face was tear streaked, her mascara running down her cheeks.

"There is one chance that you can live, Liz," Burnham told his abject, frantically fearful secretary. "Do you want to live?"

"Oh, yes, Mr. Burnham, yes, please, please don't shoot me, please!"

"And you'll do anything? Anything at all?"

"I'll do whatever you say, Mr. Burnham, I swear it, I swear!" Liz's head was pointed directly in front of her, slightly bent over, but her eyes were directed to her extreme left in an effort to receive any advanced warning of a deadly shot. Burnham stood behind her to that side. The muzzle of his pistol was at a spot just over and behind her ear. The woman's whole body cringed, not yet believing that her mortal danger had passed.

"No matter what it is?" Burnham asked, taunting her. Jake had a good idea what Burnham would want from his mature, handsome secretary. Her breasts filled her blouse well and she had slender, shapely legs. One of her shoes had come off and he could see the graceful turn of her foot. Her nylons made her legs all the more appealing, giving them a shear, smooth, tantalizing look. Jake chided himself. There had been absolutely no risk that Burnham was going to shoot the poor woman. Aside from any other reason, it was doubtful that he would have wanted to spoil his new, expensive, hand woven rug. Second, he had brought her here because he needed her. He just wanted to break her down, get her to abase herself. He wanted her to live her days in utter and complete fear of him.

"Yes, Mr. Burnham, yes, yes!" Liz pleaded desperately in answer to Burnham's last question.

"Then get on your feet, Liz," the tall, heavyset man told her. Burnham was dressed in a pair of beige slacks, dark brown, shiny, leather shoes and a light pastel green, collared knit shirt. It was incongruous to see him in his country club attire holding a pistol over a well dressed, conservatively attired businesswoman. The men who had brought Liz in had watched Burnham's charade with amusement. They had known what was coming from the getgo. They were dressed in black colored t-shirts with a red logo over the left breast. Jake hadn't noticed it until now, but it was the angry head of the mastiff that was Burnham's heraldic symbol of his estate. They wore cam-ouflage pants and thick, black, work boots. As most of the men here, they had jet black hair and scraggly beards, as if there was some local rule that you could only shave every few days and with a dull razor at that.

Burnham stepped back and then maneuvered himself in front of the tearful woman, his face about six inches from hers. She was standing there, her hands at her sides nervously clasping and unclasping. Her legs seemed to wobble. The stocking was torn on her right knee.

"Put your hands on your head, Liz," Burnham ordered in a soft, but stern voice. Liz complied obediently, a field of worry across her face. She had pledged to do anything. She was now going to find out what 'anything' was. Jake sat back down in his chair. It was like watching a train wreck. His head told him that he should not lend even his tacit consent to the destruction of this woman's personality, but his cock told him to stay.

Burnham smiled wanly at the woman and then stepped back until he was leaning against the front of his desk, his ass just over the top. "You know, Liz," he told the woman, "I've always wondered what your tits looked like under those very staid but fashionable blouses you wore. In New York, I couldn't ask you to show them to me for fear you'd scream harassment. But I think that I'd like to see them now. Please take off your jacket and your blouse."

Liz looked stunned. "What the fuck did she think 'anything' meant?" Jake asked himself.

Liz's eyes darted around at the other men in the room. She took in the naked forms of the crouching, blond girl and the unhappy, black haired girl in the cage. A look of misery crossed her face. "P,please, Mr. Burnham, please don't make me do this," she whined dismally.

"You're not going back on your promise already, Liz, are you?" Burnham asked her in a mocking tone. He still had the pistol in his hand and he gestured with it at the woman. "Let's just get on with it, Liz, before I change my mind."

Liz was still standing with her hands on her head. She slowly began to lower them. Her upper teeth were biting her lower lip in anguish.

"Oh, and one more thing, Liz," Burnham interrupted her. "On my estate, women don't talk unless they're spoken to. So just keep your mouth shut and do as you're told, okay?"

Mumbling a distraught 'yes', Liz, moving her hands slowly, began to remove her clothes. She looked around for where to place her neatly pressed, tailored jacket and when no one stepped up to help her, reluctantly let it fall to the floor about two feet away from her. She then began to unbutton her thin, white blouse. It was almost sheer and, where it touched her skin, a glimpse of veiled, tanned flesh could be seen. Summer wear.

One by one, Liz's fumbling fingers undid the buttons on her blouse. When she was done, she removed each of her thin, but well formed arms from its confines and dropped it to join the discarded jacket. For a moment, she stood looking at Burnham, sitting on the front of his desk not two feet away.

"Very nice, Liz," he said. "Keep going."

Liz's bra was a lacy white. The undersides of her breasts were covered by a thin, taut, encasement of sparkling white cotton, stretched to full, and the top halves were obscured by thin lace, just over the edge of her areolas. Her breasts were plump and she had an appreciable cleavage. Jake could see where the edges of her bathing suit had been by the semicircle of white on the tops of her breasts. The rest of Liz's chest and belly were coffee colored. Her stomach was smooth and tight. Her jacket and blouse had been hiding a thin, gold belt that encircled her supple waist. Liz reached her arms behind her back and unclipped the hooks that held her bra in place. Jake admired her deftness since it was a task that he always stumbled at, back when he had to take bras off of girls. Lately, there had been no need.

Looking up at her boss, or rather, former boss and future master, Liz hesitated to pull the bra free of her breasts. She looked as if she were checking as to whether this had been just some bad, nasty joke. But it wasn't and Burnham merely nodded in encouragement. With a soft gasp, Liz let the white fabric fall away from her generous orbs and tossed it to the side.

The woman's face hung down, framed by her thick, brown, curly hair. Her visage was obscured to Jake, but her breasts were free and clear to view. They swung softly together as they were freed and then nestled to a gentle rest. Liz had taken good care of herself. The breasts were heavy and sagged just a mite, but were well rounded and firm. Her nipples were short and thick and were stiffened by fear. The alabaster whiteness surrounding them contrasted sharply with her light brown, tanned skin, making them seem all the more tender and luscious. Faint blue veins could be seen. The pale, twin orbs stood out from Liz's chest like a pair of headlights. Burnham let the woman stew for a moment in her humiliation. Then he spoke, softly.

"Very pretty, Liz. Very nice. Not as nice as I am sure they were seven years ago, but they'll keep their shape for quite a while yet. That's important, Liz, because I couldn't have a woman with all saggy breasts working for me now, could I?"

The woman murmured a response. Burnham's voice grew angry and stern. "Look at me when you're talking to me, cunt!" he yelled at her.

Liz looked up. Tears had begun again and her mouth was drawn tight in an anguished grimace. "N,no," she let out softly. Burnham lashed out at the docile woman with his right hand. The sound of the slap echoed through the room. Liz screeched, her hands flying up too late to ward off the blow to her face. She staggered and then fell at Jake's feet.

"Oooooooow! Oh god! Please don't hit me! Please!" she cried out. There was a large red mark on her left cheek.

"Shut up and get back to your feet, cunt," Burnham barked at her. "Or I'll give you another one!"

Liz, panicking, struggled to regain her feet. Her breasts swayed and tumbled against each other as she tried to rise with some dignity. When she had brought herself to her knees, she was facing Jake. She looked at him piteously. "She recognizes me," Jake thought. "She wants help, but I have none to give. This doesn't involve me."

Liz's face, lit momentarily with false hope, turned back in on itself as she received Jake's hard stare. With a whine of self pity, she pushed herself to her feet and timidly returned to her position before the callous Burnham, hands on her head, her pretty breasts raised at attention.

"Do you know what that was for, Liz?" Burnham asked the trembling woman, referring to his harsh blow to her face.

Liz, afraid to speak, shook her head 'no'.

"You have to call me 'sir', Liz. But you didn't know that, did you?"

Liz shook her head again. She looked fearfully into Burnham's face.

"There's going to be a lot of new rules, Liz," Burnham told her. "You just don't know them all yet. But you'll learn, I'm sure. Now, back to my question. I can't have a woman with saggy breasts working for me, now can I?"

"N,no sir," Liz squeaked out.

"Very good, Liz. See, you'll get it. You're smart. That's why I hired you. That and your fine, full breasts. I interviewed a number of girls for the job, but you had the best tits."

A sob escaped from Liz's mouth. She bit her lip as if to suppress the involuntary noise.

"Now, bring your pretty breasts to me, Liz," Burnham ordered. Grimacing, Liz took two small steps closer to her former employer. "Lift them up, Liz, so I can get a good look at them."

Burnham stood a head taller than Liz, who was not short. She took her hands and cupped the bottom of her breasts, lifting them so that their rock hard nipples were pointed up at Burnham's face.

"As I thought, Liz. Very nice," he said. He took her nipples between the thumb and forefinger of each hand and pinched them, at first softly, but then pressing harder and harder until the woman winced. Burnham smiled at the woman's discomfiture. "Now show your tits to my friends, Liz. You remember Jake, don't you? I'm sure he's been wondering for years what they were like. Haven't you, Jake?"

Jake was taken by surprise by Burnham's interrogatory. Until now, he had been an observer. Now he was becoming a participant. He shifted nervously in his chair.

"Sure, Mr. Burnham," he replied. "Sure I have." In fact, he had wondered about them when he first came to see Burnham in New York many years ago.

Liz had dutifully turned towards Jake and approached him. She bent over towards him and lifted her breasts to his view. They were marvelous. The areolas were surrounded by little goose bumps and a tiny wisp of hair floated from the breast on Jake's left. As if bewitched by them, he slowly took his hands and stroked their tops. He watched them ripple as his hand ran over them. He looked up into the unhappy woman's eyes. Right then he knew that he would fuck her the first chance he got. Forty or no forty, this woman was desirable and now, soon to be available. Liz recoiled slightly as she detected Jake's lust in his glance. She knew what the look in his eyes meant and her lips pressed together in a small frown.

"Enough," Burnham called out to her, "my other guests want to see too."

Liz meekly stepped over to the grinning security men. They were less bashful than Jake and Liz gave a little cry as one of them squeezed her breast hard. The other let his tongue lap across her nipples and laughed.

The tearful, half naked woman returned to her spot before her master and owner by right of conquest. There was no legal authority that would proclaim Liz as Burnham's property, to do with as he saw fit, but it would be recognized by everyone that mattered. Afraid to release her breasts, Liz stood silently awaiting further instructions. She had kicked off her other shoe when Burnham had instructed her to make the rounds of the room and she now stood in her stockinged feet. Burnham had his glass of gin and tonic in his hand and he was admiring his new property. "Please take off your skirt and panties now, Liz. I want to see the rest of you. But leave your stockings on, okay?" the cold hearted billionaire told her. He looked over at Jake.

"Have a drink, Jake, you look like you could use one," he told him. Jake got up from his chair and walked over to the desk where he poured himself a short glass of gin over ice. His passion was now well stoked. He took a gulp and returned to his seat.

Liz had lowered her hands from her breasts and was rubbing them against her waist. Her eyes pleaded with the man whom she had served for so many years, the man that she thought she had known. She was cursing herself for playing the fool and putting herself voluntarily into his trap. Her boyfriend had not wanted her to go. They had had a big fight over it and had broken up. He wanted her to be with him, but she liked Burnham's money too much. She knew that if she didn't go he would fire her. And the prospect of travel to a seemingly exotic country had enthralled her. But now, no one at home waited for her phone call; she was isolated from her family and no one would miss her. What would she do now, she thought. What would she do now? What was going to become of her?

Sensing that Burnham was losing his patience, Liz unzipped the side of her taut, tan skirt. It slid down easily over her hips, revealing finely tanned thighs and a pair of ivory white, bikini style, silk panties. Jake could see the hair of her brown bush peaking out of the sides of the small garment. Unlike younger girls, Liz had not taken to trimming her pubic hairs and they provided a small area of padding below the woman's naval. She was wearing self supporting stockings and the lacy band at the tops clung tightly around her well formed thighs. Once the skirt was tossed aside, Liz hooked her thumbs into the waistband of the underwear and looked again at her boss. She was fighting the urge to speak, to beg, to plead. Her lips trembled and her body shook, making her breasts shimmer. Then, in one, rapid movement, she had her undergarment down below her knees. When she bent over to step out of them, her breasts swung free of her body, hanging below her chest like ripe fruit. She remained bent over for a moment, drawing out the presentation of her secret places to this cruel man. With a sob, she returned to her standing position.

"Ahhhhhhhh," Burnham exclaimed, "worth the wait!" He chuckled. "Liz, you've been holding out on me. You're a real nice piece of ass. Turn around, put your hands on your head."

Giving a mournful sigh, Liz placed her hands on top of her head and turned her body in a circle. There was a small strip of white flesh across her lower belly and on the cheeks of her back side. Her tan was definitely natural, gotten on some Caribbean isle, no doubt. The flesh of her rear quivered as she turned. She would lose those five pounds that she always wanted to very soon. Burnham's trainers would see to that. And her ass would be marked with red stripes, too. The frantically disturbed woman really had no idea what she faced.

"You'll make a fine slut, Liz. Some of the men will undoubtedly prefer, from time to time, your mature physique to that of our standard fare," he told the sobbing woman as she came to a halt.

It was the first direct statement of what her future held. If only there was something that she could do, she thought despondently. She was naked and alone in a far away country, surrounded by callous, hard men intent on her despoliation. There was nowhere to run, nowhere to hide. Her throat constricted and her belly tightened. "What am I going to do?" she wondered miserably.

The large man stepped up to the naked woman. He ran his hands down her sides, over her hips and down her thighs. Taking her by the elbows, he spun her around so that her back was pressed up against him. He grabbed her breasts from behind and caressed them. Liz suffered his touch unhappily, but did not resist.

Burnham, sliding a hand down her taut, tanned belly, reached between her thighs and insinuated his hand over her hidden nether lips. "Spread your legs, Liz, that's the girl," Burnham said to her teasingly. She was facing the leering eyes of the Russians and Jake could see the mortification in her face. It was something she would have to get over. She gasped as Burnham found his mark and pressed his thick finger inside her cleft. "Ohhhhhhhhhh!" she moaned in unhappy reaction as he forced it in deeper.

"I'm going to fuck you, Liz, but I need to get you wet first," Burnham told the naked woman. He stepped back, pulling her with him until he was back at the front of his desk.

"In a moment, my men will take you downstairs where you'll receive your training. You have some skills to perfect, Liz, and I wouldn't want you to fall short of expectations. But now, I'm going to get you started in your new duties."

Liz made a little squeal of protest when Burnham lifted her up onto the desk. He pushed her to her back and she lay across it, her back resting on Burnham's desk pad and all its presumably important papers. He lifted her legs and, grasping her stocking clad ankles, spread them widely apart.

All that could be seen of the handsome, middle aged woman was her raised knees, her tempting, spread thighs and the crevasse between them. The elastic tops of her self-supporting stockings were of dark brown lace and accentuated her tanned skin.

Burnham nudged with his foot the small blond girl who had been kneeling crouched over at the side of his desk since before Liz's ordeal began. "Get up, slut," he said to her. The girl quickly rose up and stood, her head bowed, in front of her master. "I want you to lick this cunt until it's nice and wet for me, you hear?"

"Yes, master," the pretty, piquant girl replied in a lightly accented English. She was about 5'2" tall and was dwarfed by Burnham's size. Her breasts were round and firm and she had a curvaceous shape. Her long blond hair fell to her waist behind her. She quickly insinuated herself between the prone woman's thighs and bent her head to her task. Burnham motioned Jake to come close to the desk so that he could watch.

Liz moaned in protest when she felt the blond woman's shoulders rub up against her thighs. She tried to close them as the girl applied her lips to her vulnerable and exposed sex. She sighed as the tongue began to explore the narrow slit at the entrance to her womb.

"No, no, Liz," Burnham corrected her. "Keep those sexy legs spread wide, my dear. I want you good and sopping when I stick my cock in you." Burnham placed his hand on Liz's right thigh, pulling it open. He nodded to Jake who, understanding his instruction, did the same to the left.

Liz's hands were over her face as she tried to hide her degradation. Her breasts swayed as she twisted her torso in frustrated agony. "Ohhhhhh, please, don't do this, Mr. Burnham, please!" she whined.

Burnham reached out his free hand and encircled Liz's breast. "Shhhh, Liz," he whispered. "Soon your pussy will be all hot and moist and you can enjoy my cock."

Jake watched as the nimble tongue of the young, blond girl began to excite the unhappy woman. Her face was buried in Liz's muff, but he could see her head move as she lapped at the woman's trough. The two tough looking security guards had stepped closer to get a good look at the American woman's humiliation.

The only sounds in the room was Liz's frustrated whine and the heavy breathing of the blond girl. She had encircled Liz's thighs with her arms and was working assiduously to bring the woman to lust. One of the guards placed his hand between her legs and Jake saw her spread her own thighs to accommodate him. His cock was as hard as steel as he witnessed Liz's debasement. Her face was hidden by her arms, but he could see the tell tale redness emerging on her chest, the hardening of her nipples.

Liz's breath began to become labored and rough. Her hands clenched tight into fists and she began to moan with forced passion. "Please don't, please," she murmured. But her body gave lie to expressions of dismay. Her hips began to grind back at the ardent mouth between her thighs; her hands flew down to the head of the woman who was driving her to lust. "Oh, god, please, ohhhhhhhhh!" she moaned.

Burnham took the blond girl by the hair at the back of her head and pulled her back from her task. "I think she's wet enough," he said, a smile on his lips. He had released his cock from its cage and was stroking it slowly. He moved his bulk between the moaning woman's legs and addressed himself to her moist, lush crevasse. Liz had recovered some of her equilibrium due to the cessation of the oral manipulation of her hot canal and moaned loudly when she felt the tip of Burnham's cock rub along the line of her distended slit. "Ohhhhhhhhh! Noooooooooo! Please, please, don't," she called out.

She tried to rise from her prone position, but Burnham grabbed her wrists with one of his large hands and pinned them to the desk. "Oh, Liz," he said, "I've waited a long time for this. Thank you for coming all the way out here to Kalikastan so I could fuck you." He laughed at his taunting barb.

It was with some effort that Burnham was able to pin Liz's frantically twisting hips to the desktop. He pushed his rigid cock past the entrance to her womb, sighing as her flesh enveloped him. "Oh, yeah, Liz. You've got a hot cunt. Oh, yeah!" he called out. His eyelids were closed and his eyes rolled back in their sockets as he sank deep within the unhappy woman. When he began his strokes, Liz's passionate response began anew.

"Oh! Oh! Oh! Oh!" she responded to each deep thrust of Burnham's cock. Her breasts fluttered as her body reacted to each lustful plunge. Her thighs closed tightly around the big man's torso. As her crisis approached, her body began to twist and turn, rebelling against the inevitable explosion that was to come. "No! No! No!" she cried and then "Ahhhhhhhhhhh!" as the first throb of her orgasm overcame her. Her hips thrust back at Burnham's and her back arched. "Ahhhhhhh! Ahhhhhhhhhhhhh!" she cried out.

Burnham's own orgasm loomed. "Yeah, Liz, yeah!" he yelled as his loins burned with need. "Yeah! Yeah! Arrrrrgh!" he called out as he came. He was bent over the supine form of the shapely, convulsing woman and he leaned forwards to capture her mouth with his. She spread her lips to receive him and their bodies clamped together tightly.

Jake was standing by and he admired the passionate responses of the older woman. "She'll fit in here well," he thought.

As Burnham's thrusts slowed, he separated his lips from the former free and independent woman. He stood and withdrew his softening cock from her. She lay there, moaning in the aftermath of her orgasm and in humiliation at her own licentiousness. Burnham zipped himself back up. He grabbed Liz by the hair and pulled her back from her perch on the desk to her feet. "Owwwww!" she cried as her scalp was stretched painfully.

The woman's naked body still showed the remnants of her passion and Burnham's cum was leaking down one of her thighs, smearing over the lacy top of her stocking. Her eyes were red rimmed and her hair was a tangle of knots. Burnham pulled her to the center of the room. "Put you hands on your head, slut," he commanded her. Liz obeyed, her face recording her fear and unhappiness. Burnham leaned over and picked up her silken panties from the floor. "Open your mouth," he ordered her.

With a whine of dismay, the woman parted her lips. Burnham shoved the pretty panties inside. "You talk too much, Liz. From now on, every time you talk out of turn, you'll be beaten." He looked at the two security men. One of them had taken a seat and had the blond girl draped over his lap. His hand was in her quim and she was moaning lightly. "Grab her arms," Burnham told them. The men leapt to their task and soon had Liz's arms tightly held in theirs. Burnham told the blond girl to come near him. He grabbed her and presented her to the distraught Liz. The girl's name was tattooed over her chest in florid, two inch high, bright blue lettering, and an etched in, black, red fanged mastiff, stood out prominently on her taut, lower belly. "Here's how you will be marked, Liz," Burnham said maliciously. "You're name, your slave name that is, will be tattooed across your chest just like this. And you'll receive the mark of my estate on your belly."

Liz looked at the girl's markings, her eyes spread open wide as if in disbelief. Her knees sagged and the security men had to hold her up.

"That's what you are now, Liz, a slave. And I own you. If you're obedient, and as long as I can derive some physical pleasure from you, you'll stay here and work for me like before. But if you falter, or if you should lose your charms, I will sell you to a whorehouse down in the capital."

The woman's eyes teared as she took in her fate. She murmured something, some mild protest, muffled by the dainty fabric in her mouth.

"I told you not to talk, Liz," Burnham shot out angrily. "I see that you're going to have to learn that lesson the hard way." The cruel billionaire stepped over to a tall, narrow wicker basket in the corner of the room. He pulled out of it a long, thin, rattan cane.

"I'm going to whip your tits, Liz. I'm happy that you gave me the opportunity."

The newly enslaved woman tried to break free of the security men's embrace but to no avail. They pushed her forwards so that her breasts jutted out, ready to receive their blows. The cane whistled through the air and struck the woman's breasts across their tops.

"Ooooooooooooo!" Liz moaned through her gag, her body shuddering with the blow. A second stroke hit her across her thick, short nipples. "Ooooooooooooo!" she called out. Her face grimaced with the pain. Her eyes pleaded for surcease, but Burnham had one more blow to give. He repeated the stroke across the distraught woman's nipples. She moaned, a deep, guttural moan of surrender.

Burnham tossed the whip to the side and took a deep breath. "I enjoyed that, Liz. Next time it will be five."

Long, red marks lay across Liz's fine breasts. Her face was wet with her tears and her melted mascara gave her an eerie look. Burnham knelt down before the sobbing woman and withdrew her stockings from her legs. When he stood, he said, "We'll have to get you new ones, Liz, but I think I have a use for these." He ordered the men to turn the woman around. Burnham tied one of the stockings to one of Liz's wrists and then mated the other to it. Her hands were tied effectively behind her back. The billionaire reached down and pulled Liz's glittery, golden belt from her skirt. He circled it around her neck and drew it tightly against her throat like a leash. He handed the end of the belt to one of the guards.

"Take her downstairs," Burnham said. "Tell them I want her ready in a week."

The security men nodded. Jake could see the hot passion in their eyes and he guessed that Liz would soon be getting acquainted with their hardened cocks. He would wait and try her out at his leisure.

The men started to drag the woman to the door. Her legs had given out and her toes dragged across the carpet. One of the men held her up and the other one slapped her across the face twice. "Stand up you slut!" he yelled. Terrified, Liz cried out and stiffened her legs. The man pulled her by her leash.

"Oh, by the way," Burnham called out. The men stopped and turned the woman's body so that she faced her master. "You're new slave name is Betty. The woman you knew as Liz no longer exists. I never did like that name anyway."

Liz, now Betty, didn't react to this news. It was just one more measure of abuse. The men took the naked, bound, finely tanned and curvaceous woman from the room. Burnham looked over at Jake. "Good show, eh?" he asked him, smiling.

"Not bad," Jake replied. In fact it had been damned good. Jake pledged to fuck the next slave girl that he saw.

"Why don't you take Christine here to one of the guest bedrooms and get off?" Burnham suggested. "I've got some calls to make."

Jake looked over the nubile body of the young blond girl. She looked submissively back at him, a hint of randiness in her eyes. It was a no brainer.

CHAPTER EIGHT
JACKIE, THE PONY GIRL

When the tall, muscular, grey haired man pulled the leather hood over Jackie's face, it was as if the whole world changed at once. Her vision was limited to two vertical slits in the hood. The world had suddenly become very small. Her gag was removed and, before she could resist, a leather covered, steel bit was inserted instead. Jackie ground her teeth on it in unhappy frustration. The man pulled her over to a full length mirror on the wall.

"Look at the nice ponygirl," he said in Russian to the room. Once a slave became a ponygirl, it was standard practice never to address her directly other than to issue short, curt commands. The other men in the room laughed. Jackie certainly knew the tenor of what the man said. She looked at the grotesque simulacrum of a woman reflected before her. She could see that it was her; she knew she was standing in front of a mirror. But it was not her, not the person she had been. The head was obscured by the coarse, leather hood, her lips were stretched and distended by the bit. She had no eyes and no face. Her pubic hair was gone and her cleft was surrounded by clean, hairless, fleshy lips. She also had no arms, they being rudely tied off behind her. Her naked breasts looked back at her mournfully, the areolas standing out as dark, sad eyes. And then there was the collar. It was thick and heavy and it had bright, brass rings dangling from it. Her upper body was outfitted with a leather harness. No, she was not a human being any more. She was a ponygirl.

After affixing heavy, black boots to her feet, the men clipped a leash to a ring in the front of her collar and made

Jackie strut around the room. She was overwhelmed with fear and sorrow. She had done this to herself. That was the worst of it all. Jake had said it would be hard and she had not really believed him. What could be harder than hooking in Chicago? Well, this could. Tears flowed down Jackie's face inside her hood. They were tears of anger and sadness. She was angry at what these white men were doing to her. She wanted to kick out at them with her heavy boots, make them cry out in pain. Her sadness came as she realized her utter powerlessness. These men could do anything they wanted with her.

After being led around the room several times, Jackie was brought back to the mirror. Her legs were forced apart. A hand snaked in from behind her and covered her hairless pussy. She jumped at the callous handling of her flesh. She struggled to close her legs, but they were locked apart by the feet of the other men. The man with the grey hair was behind her. She could see glimpses of his leering face in the mirror through the slits in her hood. The hand that had seized her loins started to rub it gently, tickling the outer skin, running a finger down the narrow slit. Jackie rebelled against her handling, trying to break free but the men held her fast. She felt her cleft moistening as the rough, strong hand of the grey haired man continued to manipulate it.

The man was patient. There was no rush, after all. The pony trailer wouldn't be here for several hours. And stroking a new ponygirl to orgasm was fun.

The fingers of the hand now slid easily between Jackie's distended, engorged nether lips. Her moisture covered it. Jackie could smell her own arousal intermingled with the unmistakable smell of polished leather. Her back was pressed against the man's chest and her useless hands were touching his hard, muscled stomach. She tried to loosen her knees so that she could sink down, frustrating the insistent hand. But the man held her up, his free arm around her waist, forcing her to watch her own debasement.

Sure, Jackie had given herself to many men. She had sucked their cocks and let them kiss and fondle her chocolate pussy. But this was something different. The johns had never really touched her, she remained aloof, and mostly, in control. The hand that tantalized her cunt now seemed to reach deep inside her, making contact with her inner being, defiling everything that she had been. And, she was definitely not in control.

The men became amused as Jackie came closer and closer to completion. Her dripping pussy was burning with lust in spite of herself. She was lost in the reverie of a preorgasm swoon and she unconsciously rocked her hips, enticing the hand to go faster, stronger. But the man had his own pace. She was to come at his command and at no other time. His pale hand stood in contrast to her dark brown colored skin and Jackie could discern its workings in the mirror through the narrow strips in her hood.

"Ooooooompf! Oooooooompf!" Jackie exclaimed as she felt her blood begin to boil. Her whole body jerked in rebellion against its forced pleasure. "Ooooooompf! Ooooooompf!" she cried, her attempt at words being muffled and distorted by the cruel bit. When she felt her pussy begin to throb, she pressed it down hard on the hand that tormented her, jerking and convulsing where she stood. Her mind clouded as the throes of her orgasm tore through her.

Not satisfied at one orgasm, the hand continued its manipulations until Jackie's blood was on the boil again. "Ooooooooompf! Oooooooooompf!" she cried as the second series of heavy, body shaking throbs went through her. When the newly minted ponygirl had crested for the third time, her voice screeching out from behind her bit, her legs pumping madly, the hand finally withdrew.

Jackie slumped in the man's arms. Slowly, she returned to consciousness from her sex befogged state. She realized that one of the men had seized one of her ample, brown breasts and was squeezing it tightly. The men all laughed when she whined at the painful caress.

The new ponygirl was led outside by her leash. She knew that she was in the men's power and that resistance was futile. She was guided to a post near the stairs to the upper level, and the back of her collar was tied off to a ring. Her legs were forced widespread by tying off rings in her boots to large steel rings embedded in the earth. She was left alone for a long time. Twice, the comely, naked, young women from inside the barracks came streaming out of the door and ran crazed around the cobblestone courtyard. Their hands were bound behind them and they wore their gags in their mouths. Silently, their bare chests rising and falling with their deep breaths, their breasts flying to and fro, they made the rounds as lounging men yelled and clapped to them. They all glanced fearfully at Jackie as they passed by her, afraid lest they meet a fate similar to hers. When they had shuffled back into the barracks, all was silent again.

After a while, Jackie felt the presence of someone next to her. She turned her head. Although her vision was limited by the hood to what she could see through the narrow slits, she saw that it was one of the men who she had assaulted in her escape attempt. Her skin crawled as the man placed his hand on her breast and caressed it. He was smiling ear to ear and Jackie had a premonition that he was going to harm her in some way. He squeezed the plump orb and murmured something in a foreign tongue in Jackie's ear. Jackie tried to pull away from him, but the short chain linking the rear of her collar to the post prevented it as did the bindings on her spread ankles.

Once the man had satisfied himself with caressing her soft, naked, brown breast, he stepped back and removed a small jar of ointment from his pocket. There was also a rubber surgical glove. He placed it on his right hand and then, after opening the jar, took a large dollop of ointment on his gloved fingers. He smiled evilly at Jackie. Whatever the ointment was, Jackie wanted no part of it. She shook and pulled at her bindings, howling into her bit in anguished frustration. Her hands strained at their bindings. "You bastard! You bastard!" she yelled, but the sounds that emerged were more like, "Ooo-a-er! Ooo-a-er!"

The man laughed at the naked, brown skinned girl's distraught reactions. He held out his gloved hand and pressed the ointment into and along Jackie's exposed slit. The gel acted as a lubricant and he was able to force his gloved fingers in a long way. When he had distributed the ointment over and in Jackie's sex and over her large pleasure bud, he withdrew his hand. He laughed again and, after making some caustic statement in Russian, walked away.

At first, the only reaction that Jackie had to the ointment was the cool air that flowed over it. For a few moments, she began to believe that the ointment had some benign purpose and that her fearful reactions had been unwarranted. But, slowly the skin that was in contact with the ointment began to tingle. Then the tingling became an irritant. And then it began to burn.

"Ooooooooooh! Ooooooooooh!" Jackie screamed as her loins felt as they were on fire. "Ooooooooh! Ooooooooooh!" she screamed. She had never felt anything like it. It was as if a thousand needles were penetrating her pussy's walls and the soft skin of her nether lips. She danced in place, writhing her hips, trying desperately to bring her thighs together. For the next twenty minutes, Jackie's whole consciousness was directed to the agonizing pain in her loins. All of her thoughts were directed at the naked slit between her thighs and the need for relief from the awful sensations. From time to time, one of the workmen would pass by and Jackie would beg and plead, insofar as she was able, for mercy, for help. "Eeeeeease! Eeeeeeease! El eeee!" The bit prevented Jackie from forming any hard consonants as she was unable to bring her lips together. Her distorted words were like a new, alien language, indecipherable to the human ear. But the men knew what she was going through. Serge had ordered it and Alexi, the man whom Jackie had kicked in the balls, had told everyone how pissed he was at the new ponygirl and how he would get back at her. Men smiled and laughed as they passed, noting the jiggling of Jackie's large breasts as she contorted her body.

After the first twenty minutes, the burning sensation began to subside. Tears flowed down Jackie's imprisoned face from her ordeal. Her body felt drained of energy. But the sensations brought on by the invidious ointment did not go away fully. The burning sensation had turned to an irritating itch. The ponygirl yearned to feel some touch on her pussy, to have it probed to relieve the mind bending obsession. Her hips circled in frustration as her empty channel begged for contact. One man came close and tickled her nipples for a few moments. He noted her proffered loins and smiled. He ran a finger along the edges of Jackie's hairless slit, smiling at her. Jackie reveled at the contact, but wanted more, much more. Her whole body begged the man to place his hand on her cunt, to probe her chasm. But the man only smiled and stroked lightly the outer lips.

A few minutes after the man left, the girls from the barracks came out for another run. Whistles blew and men called out as the silenced and bound women made their circumnavigation of the courtyard. Jackie found herself envying these distressed, naked women. Although their hands were bound behind them and their mouths gagged, they could see and they had hair. They were still, nominally at least, people. And whatever their destiny, it did not involve the intentional depersonalization that she had undergone and would under go. As abject as their own fates would be, Jackie wanted to be one of them, to be part of the crowd. As the breathless women made their way back into the barracks, her heart ached with self pity.

When the sun sank just behind the westward roof of the compound, a battered, dark blue, pickup truck entered the courtyard through the large gateway. It was towing a dusty, silver, horse trailer behind it. Jackie's stomach roiled as she realized that it was for her. Her pussy's torment had subsided to a barely tolerable level by now, although she would have welcomed a hard cock inside her. When the pickup rounded the yard and pulled the trailer straight behind it, the engine was turned off and a man jumped out. He was dressed in scruffy, blue jeans and a tattered, black t-shirt. He wore a thick, nascent beard and roughly cut, black hair down over his ears. There were thick, black work boots on his feet.

Jackie heard steps on the stairs behind her. It was Khalid and the grey haired man. They welcomed the driver with shouts.

"You're late, you son of a camel," Khalid called to the man in Russian.

"So what, you fat piece of horse dropping!" the man called back. "I had a problem at a checkpoint. If I didn't have this pass, I would have been picking lead from my liver by now."

Although the country was divided up into the interests of numerous gangs, a pass to Khalid's brought universal respect. No one was permitted to interfere with the market in ponygirls or slave girls.

Khalid and Serge, the grey haired man, stopped when they were abreast of Jackie. The other man approached and shook their hands.

"So this is the new ponygirl," the man said in Russian. "A chocolate beauty," he remarked.

"Yes, and a very rebellious one," Khalid answered. "She'll be tough to break, but damn sure worth it when it's all done. As my men can tell you, she's fast and strong. She almost jumped over the compound wall after escaping from the control of two of my men. What a waste of good ponyflesh that would have been. She would've been crushed on the rocks below. She was saved just in time."

The driver of the van proceeded to run his hands over Jackie's body. He felt the strength of her thighs and shoulders, the heft of her breasts, the smoothness of her naked crevasse. Jackie sighed when the man placed his fingers along her long slit. The man laughed. "She's practically broken in already!" he said. "She's hot at the first touch."

"No, I had one of men do that," Khalid answered. "She's been dancing all afternoon here as a result of a cream my man put on her pussy as a punishment. She's still sensitive there. I'd bet she would gladly fuck all of us twice right now." All three of the men laughed.

"Well, let's get her aboard," the driver said. "It's a long drive and I want to get there before dawn."

The steel eyed man with the short, buzz cut, gray hair knelt at Jackie's feet. He unhooked one ankle and affixed one end of a chain to the boot. He then loosened the other and connected the two ankles together. It was a short chain, about 18 inches in length. Jackie wouldn't be running anywhere.

The clip holding Jackie's collar to the post was released. Desperate not to be loaded into the pony trailer, Jackie pulled back when Serge fixed his finger in the front ring of her collar to pull her along. He moved with lightning quickness as he lashed out with his free hand and struck her across her breasts twice. She was stunned by the blows and called out, "Oooooooooooh!" The gray haired man pulled her closer to him by the ring on her collar and leered into the small slits in her hood. Jackie could see his soulless, shark's eyes. She realized that resistance was hopeless. These men would get her in the van one way or another. What was the use of fighting it?

Jackie dutifully followed the grey haired man across the courtyard, advancing with little steps made necessary by her confined ankles. The dirty, silver, pony trailer was close to the ground and it was easy to get Jackie up into it. She trembled with dread as her ankles were affixed to rings in the floor and her waist put up against and bound to a bar across the width of the trailer. A chain was pulled from a hook on the wall in front of her and locked to her collar. It was pulled tight, forcing Jackie to bend forward slightly. With a loud slap on her rump, the driver stepped out of the trailer and, after shaking Khalid's and Serge's hands, got back into the truck. He started the engine and pulled the pickup to the gate. When it opened, he drove through.

Jackie was miserable in her confines. She realized that she was being treated as an animal, that the driver and the other men at the compound no longer considered her a person. The diver had been happy to examine her thighs and back, the strength of her shoulders, but cared not a whit for her face. As a whore, Jackie had taken great care of her face. After the tits, it was the second thing the men looked at. She knew she had great tits, but without a great face to match it, she would have been giving blow jobs in the front seats of the cars of commuter johns. But now her face was of absolutely no interest to anyone. Jake had said that she would be hooded for months. She didn't know if she could stand it. She could only hope that she would see

Jake soon and that he would convince these ruthless and cruel men to release her.

The trip was uneventful. Twice, during the night, the man gave her water to drink and let her pee on the side of the road. Jackie contemplated making a run for it, but the man held her by a chain connected to her collar and where would she go anyway? Without a way to undo her bound wrists and remove her accouterments, she would just be an escaped ponygirl. She couldn't see worth a damn and she was gagged. Taking into account the trouble they had taken to get her here, she was sure there would be a reward to turn her in. No, she would have to wait for a better opportunity.

They arrived at the Burnham estate about a quarter after eight in the morning. Jackie had slept fitfully during the night. Leaning against the rail, her legs spread, her neck pulled forward, she would doze off on occasion. She would have strange, foreboding dreams of being confined, being held prisoner. Men leered at her and mocked her. When she awoke, at first, she was happy to be free from the torments of her psyche. But then she would realize where she was. In the darkness that surrounded her, she could hear and feel the whir of the tires on the road, feel the sway of the van as it made turns. At times, her terror and despair got the better of her and she yanked and pulled at her bonds, screaming into the darkness through her distended mouth. When her fit had passed, she would rest her waist on the rail across the width of the van and sob and cry. Soon afterwards, she would fall asleep and restart the cycle of nightmare, awakening, rage and then piteous submission.

The driver pulled the van up the long driveway to Burnham's estate and along in front of the mansion. He was tired, thirsty and hungry. He walked down to the trainer's bunkhouse for breakfast. He left Jackie where she was. It didn't matter to him whether she ate or not, whether she had to pee or not. His job was done.

Burnham had been up since six o'clock, reading the overnight financial reports. He liked to sit at the breakfast table in the large, well equipped kitchen, his cock in the mouth of a nubile slave girl kneeling between his legs. Her job was to transfer the soothing warmth of her mouth to his soft dick, not to excite him or to bring him to pleasure. When he was done eating, and by then his cock had usually grown to rock hard, he bent the slave girl over the table and finished himself in her ass or her cunt, as the whim took him.

At 8 o'clock, he was well past that. He was dressed and at his desk. At nine, he took his morning peramble with Dora and Flora. He loved watching the cream white flanks of the ponies as they plied the country roads surrounding his estate. He had the grooms apply a strong sunscreen to their bodies to ensure that they maintained their pale complexions. At ten, when he returned, he would turn the large, white ponies over to Tucker who would rub them down and fuck them.

This morning, he had a special task. Every time a new pony was brought on to the estate, it was his right and duty to ceremonially claim it as his own. He would make sure that it saw his face, the face of its master and owner, and then rape it with his rock hard, thick cock. The men usually gathered round and he enjoyed showing off his virility in front of them. They were a rough, hard lot, and he wanted to be known as being as rough and as hard as any of them. He wanted, and needed, to prove that he held no scruples regarding the nation's premier sport. The fact of the matter was that he reveled in the ownership of female flesh. He had never dreamed it could be so good.

Jackie stood in her van, bound and gagged as the morning wore on. The need to pee became overwhelming and eventually, to her dismay, she let go right where she stood. It didn't matter. Stock animals could not be held to account for where they pissed. The van would be hosed out later by one of the grooms.

Several times, Jackie heard voices behind her as men came by to get a glimpse of the new ponygirl. The rumor had it that she was special, bought to run, not as a yearling, but to challenge the supremacy in the 1500 meter sulky race of last spring's champion, Lightning, owned by the Grobgy estate. There were few secrets regarding ponygirls.

One of the people who stuck their heads in the van was Jake. He wanted to see how the poor, young whore was doing. He knew that nothing he could have said would have prepared her for the experience of becoming a ponygirl and he constantly blamed himself for getting her involved. Although Jackie heard Jake open the rear flap of the van, she did not see who it was. She was able to turn her head slightly, but she had no peripheral vision, so the most that she could see was the side of the van. But Jake could see her, her writhing hands imprisoned behind her back, the obligatory pony tail and the cruel bit in her mouth. "Look what I've done," he said to himself.

At about 10:15, Jackie was released from the van. One of the grooms had come to get her. She followed him docilely out of the trailer. She was amazed to see, what little she could see, that she was in the middle of a large estate. She saw a big house, long, white, rail fences and what appeared to be a racing track. The groom tugged her along by a leash attached to her collar. After a short walk, they came up to a small building. It was the tack shop for the estate where all the harnesses and leather leads for the ponygirls were manufactured, repaired and stored. It served as a general, informal meeting place, and men could usually be found sitting on its long, broad porch bullshitting each other.

Jackie knew that something was up right away. A circle of coarsely dressed men were awaiting her. She was led up to them and the groom took her leash and held it close to her collar so that he could show her off. He lifted her neck so that she was standing on the toes of her large, black boots. She whined as the collar began to choke her. There were seemingly admiring comments from the men and one or two came up and felt her breasts or ran their hands over her thighs.

After a few moments, the men parted and a tall man with heavy, broad shoulders appeared. He was dressed smartly in comfortable, leisure clothes. He came up to her, clapping some of the other men on the back. Jackie could just see him through her hood's little slits. She saw him take the leash from the man who had unloaded her from the van and he pulled her close to him with it. He forced her face no more than inches away from his own. He said nothing, but stared deeply into her slits. His eyes were piercing, cruel, and Jackie shivered with dismay. She was in this man's power, that was clear. But was this the man, Burnham, that Jake had told her about? Or had there been some mix-up or change in plan and this was an entirely different owner? The distinction was important. If it was Burnham, she would be released in five months. If it wasn't, she would be condemned to live as a ponygirl for a long, long, time.

It was Burnham, and he took his time peering into the darkness inside the ponygirl's hood. Irkut, who was to be her trainer, emphasized the importance of not speaking English in front of the girl. Irkut knew nothing about the plan to save Maddy and so the training of Jackie would have to proceed just like any other ponygirl. After today, he would be her god, in control of every aspect of her existence, able to instill either pleasure or pain. Jackie would meet Irkut shortly.

Jackie was frightened by what she saw in the man's eyes. Burnham's or not, they were cruel eyes and Jackie shivered in fear. He turned and led her by her leash to what looked like a small hitching post that stood about waist high. He handed the leash over to the groom and he pulled the new ponygirl up against the rail. Hands from behind her spread her legs and fastened her ankles to the posts. The groom took the leash and pulled Jackie over the rail until she was bent in half. He tied off the leash to a ring that had been pounded into the ground. Jackie was no rocket scholar, but she knew right away why she had been tied thusly. She could feel her sex and rear exposed for all to see, and use, if they saw fit. She saw between her legs from her upside down position, the sharply creased, light green pants of the man who had stared into her face and his highly polished, brown, patent leather shoes. Then she felt his hand caress her naked, hairless slit.

The grotesquely bound ponygirl shivered as she felt the man's fingers trace the length of her soft divot. She felt the eyes of all the men on her body. She strained at her bindings in futile protest. The hand continued to torment her and soon her slit was slick with her fluids. The man ran his hands up and down the backs and insides of her thighs, exciting her. She knew that he had taken his prick out when she felt its bulbous head probe between her distending, swelling labia. Despite her horror at her treatment, she was being aroused by the man's exertions. Around her, the men were jesting with each other in a foreign tongue. Jake had said that they were Russians. Maybe they were. But they were callous, evil minded men as far as she was concerned, regardless of their nationality. Who else would devise a system that treated women so?

But to the men around her, Jackie was no longer a woman. She was a ponygirl and an exotic one at that. Most of the ponies were Caucasian women, stolen from the streets and homes of Europe and North America. There were other races represented, but they were few and far between. Jackie was the only African-American pony on the estate and would be the first, to anyone's memory, to be trained as a sulky pony. Jackie was making ponygirl history.

The hot, thick cock of her new owner slid along the steamy slit of Jackie's sex. Her blood had risen and she was ready to be impaled. Despite her predicament, she wanted it, wanted the man's cock up her pussy. The sensations brought on by the ointment the previous day still lingered and Jackie could not wait for somebody to scratch her itch.

But that was not Burnham's intent. He preferred to claim his ponygirls through the other, narrower entrance. Most of the new ponies had never been fucked there and it was quite a surprise to them when that path was chosen. It was the same with Jackie. She had never allowed a john or anyone else to pierce her nether place. She had always refused, no matter how much money was offered. The thought of it repelled her.

When his tool was well lubricated by Jackie's discharge, Burnham let his prick slide up the girl's perineum, trailing a line of her viscous fluids behind it. His rock hard prick stood poised at the entranceway to Jackie's bowels. She had felt the cock slip from her gushing canal to her rear and she knew at once what was planned. Panicking, the pony-girl tried to stiffen the muscles of her rear to deny the cock admittance. She would learn soon to loosen them and welcome intruders or she would suffer the consequences. But her reaction delighted Burnham as it indicated to him that no one else had ever ventured there.

The plump head of Burnham's hard prick pressed against the small, exposed ring of flesh. Eased by the ponygirl's own moisture, he was able to slip it past the tight, hard entrance and plunge within.

Jackie screamed as she felt her sphincter muscles stretched and torn. She tried to wriggle her hips and rear to expel the invader, much to the amusement of the surrounding crowd. "Oooooooh! Ohhhhhhhhhhh!" she cried from behind her bit as the pain shot through her. "Eeeeeeease! Eeeeeeeeeese!' she cried out, a sound that made the men laugh.

Burnham's eyes closed as he enjoyed the experience of the tight ring around his cock and the heat of Jackie's innards. He reached his hand under Jackie, between her legs, and was able to stroke her plush pussy in time to his strokes in her rear. He had excellent control and would wait until she had been fully and properly roused to allow his passion to overcome him.

Something went off in Jackie's brain when she felt the hand continue the job that her owner's prick had begun. She felt filled as she never had before and the sensations that she was experiencing there, behind her, were not all of pain. As the fingers excited her pleasure bud and delved into her heated canal, the ponygirl began to tremble and shake. She began to moan with pleasure. Her blood was boiling and her mind had shut out all but the rasping of the thick prick against the tender and sensitive skin of her rear entrance and the maddeningly pleasurable caresses to her pussy. "Ummmpf! Ummmmmmpf! Ummmmmmmpf!" she called out as her orgasm began. Her torso was convulsing and her breasts were shaking to and fro. There was a sheen of passion induced perspiration all over her and her skin seemed polished to a lustrous shine. "Ooooompf! Oooooompf!" she cried as her womb's tunnel began to contract and throb with pleasure.

Burnham felt it through the thin wall dividing her womb and her bowels. He smiled at the reward for his efforts and allowed the flow of his own orgasm to build within him. His hands were now both on the railing to either side of the ponygirl and he used it to propel himself hard against her rear cheeks, thrusting himself deeper and deeper inside her. When he came, he groaned loudly, jetting his hot fluids deep into her. Jackie felt the pulsing of his large cock against her anal ring and she began to come once more, shuddering and moaning.

When Jackie regained her senses, the man had already withdrawn himself from her body and was walking away. It seemed to be a general signal for the men to disburse. A couple of the men gave her sharp slaps on her behind as they passed her. The poor, former woman remained spread and bound on the rail of the hitching post. Her heart was still pounding from her fucking. Dismally, she relived her experience in her mind. She had once done a little strip-ping, but that was really for the amateurs, girls on the borderline of 'the life'. She had enjoyed having the men ogle her exposed flesh, felt ratified in the lust that she arose in them. But this was nothing like that. She had come wildly before a crowd of unknown men, men who, unlike the patrons of a strip club, could fuck her at their whim, regardless of her consent. She was sure that the show that she had put on would drive many of them to lust on her body.

She was left splayed on the hitching post for some time. Irkut, who had witnessed the ponygirl's initiation, had gone back to the house with Burnham. They were sitting in the sun room, taking some lunch. Two delicately lovely, naked, brown haired, slave girls scurried in and out with their food and drinks. From time to time one or the other of the men would absentmindedly caress their naked flanks as they delivered a plate of food, or bent over to pour a drink.

"What do you think?" Burnham asked the experienced ponygirl trainer. Irkut had been in the sport almost since when it was revived from ancient custom ten years ago. It had started out small but had grown into a major national enterprise. It had made Irkut wealthy and he had retired, but Burnham's cash had enticed him back to 'the game'.

"She's got spirit," Irkut answered him. "They tell me she almost escaped at Khalid's the other day. She has good, strong legs and a sturdy build. But she could be a clunker, all strength and no speed."

"Oh, she's fast all right," Burnham told him. "I did my homework. She was a track star in high school; ran the 5000 meter, individual and relay."

"That's very good. So she has speed," Irkut answered. "But she needs more than strength and speed. She's got to want it so badly that she'll burst her lungs trying to get it. Racing has to become her whole reason for existence. Otherwise, she doesn't stand a chance. It's for good reason that yearlings aren't usually used for the sulkies or the other teams. They're skittish and too fresh to their bits. At night they cry and moan. But the older ponies have shaken off the memories of their former lives. They know that this is their life now and they have no other. This pony will struggle hard to retain her memories of womanhood. They'll have to be driven out of her ruthlessly."

Burnham skewered a large, pink shrimp. "You're the expert," he said. "I leave it all up to you."

"Let me ask you something," Irkut inquired. "Why all the drive to win the sulky championship this year? We could work the yearlings that you bought and, along with the older ponies to show them the way, you could have a good estate team next year, maybe a contender the year after that. This new pony, if matched to the right yearling, could take that trophy this fall easily. So why should she run the sulky now?"

Burnham had prepared himself for this question, an obvious one since what Irkut was saying was the truth.

"It's a personal thing. Grobgy really got me pissed off when I met him last month, preening over his sulky champion. I want to shove it down his throat. And I want to make a name for myself now rather than later. I know that a lot of you are not pleased by my entry into the sport. All I want is to make my bones and get all that talk behind me."

Irkut paused to take this in. He had grown suspicious while on 'tour' with Jake in the spring looking at potential purchases for the Burnham barn. Jake seemed inordinately interested in yearlings during their eight week search. Then, almost right after he had seen Grobgy's pony, Lightning, run, he had called off the search for ponygirls for sale and returned to the estate. And now Burnham was talking about challenging Lightning. He could smell something untoward somewhere in this. He was patient. He would learn more before deciding what to do. In the meantime, he had a ponygirl to train.

When they had finished lunch, Irkut, declining Burnham's invitation to stay and play with their waitresses, went down to the tack shop to retrieve his new student. She was right where she had been left, as he knew she would be. He came up to her and placed his hand on her raised rump, caressing it. She had soft, brown skin, a delightful change from the pallor of most of the ponygirls. Her ass was tight and muscled. She shuddered when he touched her and moaned when he rubbed his hands over her rear. Was that a protest or an invitation, Irkut wondered.

The pony trainer stepped over to the other side of the hitching post and released the ponygirl's leash. He allowed her to stand and then, holding on to her leash, released her ankle confinements. She would do no running off while under his supervision if he could help it. He realized that the pony must be hungry and tired, but figured that this was the time to make the strongest impression on it. He guided it down to the training paddock and, opening the gate, brought her in.

The training paddock was a ring surrounded by a solid 8' high wall of white washed, corrugated steel. It was sunk about three feet below the surface of the surrounding ground so that interested persons could stand at the wall and peer down to watch the fun. But the view from inside the paddock was only sky. Its circumference was about fifty yards so there was plenty of running room. Running in too tight a circle could cause damage to the pony's ligaments and joints. The curve of the walls was slight, almost straight. Varying the direction in which they ran equalized stress on the legs.

In the middle of the paddock was a spindle-like post. Attached to it was a long, sturdy pole with a ring at its end. It was connected to a motor and turned around the paddock at varying speeds in both directions. Soon, this new pony would have her first workout on it. But there was business to attend to first.

Irkut had prepositioned a box with the pony's new raiment in the paddock area. The leather hood that the slave clearing station run by Khalid had adorned her with was primitive and not conducive to racing. It was coarse and heavy, and was important in impressing on the new pony her change in status. But Irkut needed to dress the new pony in the headgear particular to Burnham's estate, the black, Neoprene hood. He also had to replace the thick, leather collar the pony was now wearing with one better suited to pulling a carriage.

Irkut had the pony stand a couple of feet from the corrugated, white, steel wall. Without speaking to her, he undid the belt holding the bit in her mouth and then removed the leather hood. The pony tried to move her head, but Irkut grabbed her under her chin and held her head fast in a fierce grip.

Jackie felt relieved when the hood was removed. Her head had been hot and even the waft of midday air across it was refreshing. She tried to turn to face the man who had released her from the terrible hitching post where she had been confined for what seemed like hours, but felt his hard hand on her neck, his fingers grasping her lower jaw tightly. The message was unmistakable and she kept her view straight ahead. It was a relief just to be able to see clearly again. And even though all she could see was the wall of white in front of her, she delighted in her liberated vision.

The pony's delight would be short lived. Irkut next removed the pony's collar and the harness she had worn. He threw them to the middle of the ring, near the spindle post so they would be out of the way. The pony's wrists were now free of their bindings for the first time in two days. Jackie thanked providence as she swung her arms free.

Now that she was undressed, it was time to dress her properly in the equipage of her new life. First was the racing collar. Irkut pulled it out of the box and circled the pony's neck with it. Jackie jumped when she felt it applied. It raised her chin up high, eliminating any ability to look down. To see her feet, she would have to bend at the waist. The collar was close fitting and encased her chin. To look side to side, the new pony would have to twist her torso.

Immediately afterwards, Irkut took each wrist and affixed a leather bracelet to it. The bracelets connected to a strap than ran down the back of the collar to the pony's waist. The hands were kept locked low, in the small of her back. Putting them high would place undue strain on the arms and actually sometimes made them stronger. The idea was that arm strength would wither away, until the pony lost all conscious thought about them. Also, keeping the hands low made it simpler to apply a racing harness that could be affixed to leads from a carriage, helping to pull it.

When Jackie felt the leather bracelets go around her wrists, she began to cry. She had had a slight hope that the man was relieving her of the indignities of the ponygirl confinements. But he was just putting better, more restrictive ones on. She had been subdued by the experience of being hauled some long distance to this vast estate and made to perform before the crowd of men. When she realized that she would be soon losing again all chance of defending herself or escape, just as Irkut attached her left wrist to the strap behind her back, she tried to turn to push the man back and flee. But Irkut was no novice at his task. He anticipated her move and shoved her torso roughly against the coarse, steel wall. Jackie's face banged up against it and her breasts were scraped by its rough surface. Irkut expertly grabbed Jackie's free wrist and attached it to the strap behind her. No problem.

A wave of despair flowed through the unhappy ponygirl. She had been slapped for trying to talk before, but she figured that this might be her last chance. "Please...," she began to say. Irkut's right hand came around from behind her and grabbed her cheeks pressing them harshly. "Awwwwwwwg!" was all that Jackie got out after her initial word. Irkut's other hand snuck between her legs and grabbed a hold of her tender pussy lips. He squeezed them tightly, causing the pony to groan. He held the pressure for about twenty seconds. Jackie struggled to free herself, but Irkut pressed her body back up against the steel wall with his. The pony moaned with pain. After the twenty seconds had passed, Irkut slowly released his hold on the pony's pussy lips. Her body, which had been tensed, started to relax. He let go completely while keeping his other hand on her mouth, pinching her cheeks together.

Jackie surrendered. She let her body go limp as a sign of the end of her resistance. The man was too strong for her, especially since she was deprived of the use of her hands. She cursed herself for letting him rope in the first one.

Gradually, Irkut stepped back, letting Jackie stand back from the steel wall and then, just as slowly, released his cruel grip on her mouth. Jackie knew better than to try and say anything else. This man obviously didn't care anyway. Was there no one who would take mercy on her, she thought despairingly.

Once the pony had returned to her docile stance, Irkut took a black hood from his pocket and, holding it open, drew the pony's ponytail through a hole in the back. It was then a simple matter of drawing the hood over the rest of the mostly bald head until the face was fully covered, leaving a space for the pony's mouth and nostrils. The hood had snaps around its bottom which connected to snaps on the top of the collar. The pony was thus covered from the top of her head to the bottom of her collar. The snaps allowed the thick, clingy hood to be pulled taut, and prevented its accidental removal.

When the hood was fully over her head, Jackie was startled to find that her eyesight had been further reduced to what she could see through two tiny holes. The leather hood had had slits and so she could move her eyes up and down to see more of what was around her. But these holes were so small that all she would be able to see was a miniscule dot of reality. As a ponygirl, it was all she needed to see.

Irkut didn't wait for the pony to recover from the shock of her diminished eyesight. He had the gag ready and he pushed open her mouth with one hand and slid the long, thick, leather plug in without resistance. It had a shield attached which covered the lower portion of the pony's face and buckled at the back of her head.

His work being temporarily done, Irkut took the box, put the discarded hood and harness in it and kicked it to the middle of the paddock. The ponygirl was standing where he had left her, apparently overcome with her new restraints. He had carefully avoided looking into her face, because he didn't want to personalize the former woman under the hood. She now looked like the two dozen or so other ponies on the estate. She still lacked her tattoos, but they would come later. "I have to come up with a good name for her," he thought to himself. He had no clue as to her former name and didn't care.

The former Jackie was overwhelmed by the new hood and collar that she was wearing. With the leather hood, it had been clear that she had been wearing something foreign over her head, something separate and apart from her. But this new hood seemed just like another layer of skin. It was tight and light. She almost couldn't feel it on her face. But the two little dots of light in front of her eyes reminded her that it was there.

She turned to look at her tormentor. It took her a moment to find him using the small holes in her hood. She wanted to beg and plead with him to release her. She uttered a long, low moan and sank to her knees. Her face was a mask of agony and fear. But Irkut couldn't see it. Her head was devoid of all expression. She might as well have been a faceless manikin.

Jackie sat back on her haunches and cried. Even her sobs were muffled by the cruel gag. The hood quickly absorbed her tears. "What is to become of me?" she thought, in despair at her plight. "How can I stand it?"

But she would have to stand it. Pain was a great motivator and ponygirl trainers considered the whip as secondary in importance only to food. Jackie had not yet experienced the whip. She had seen it used at Khalid's, but seeing it and experiencing it were two different things.

Irkut had a good idea what the new pony was going through and paused to let her fate sink in. He took out a white tube of black, Russian tobacco and lit it. He was at the opposite side of the paddock from the pony and he leaned against the wall, admiring her rising and falling, plump breasts, the beautiful color of her skin. Whatever Burnham's game was, he was glad of the opportunity to train such a luscious, spirited pony.

He finished his cigarette and field stripped it. It would not due to litter the interior of the training paddock. The dirt in it was soft and clayey like the dirt of a baseball diamond. It could be raked smooth and was after each training session. Irkut would not have sole use of the training paddock with so many yearlings about.

Having finished his smoke, Irkut went over to the wall where hung a variety of whips. There was a thick riding crop, a long, rattan cane, a flogger and a pony whip. Irkut selected the pony whip, a long handled whip with a long, thin lash of twisted leather. It had a braid at the end for special emphasis. It was time to teach the ponygirl her first lesson.

Jackie saw the man approaching with the whip. She looked at him with dread. She was too frightened to move. But when he snapped the whip at her the first time, catching her high on her shoulder, just down her back, she cried out and, in panic, rose to her feet to escape it. This was, of course, what Irkut wanted and expected.

The pain burned through Jackie's skin. She looked back at the man in disbelief. He was going to whip her! She ran to the other side of the paddock, but the man followed her. He threw the long, thin tassel at her again, catching her on her left thigh. It was like a hornet's sting and Jackie cried out in pain. She ran and she ran, but there was no place to hide. Again and again he struck her. Each time, the ponygirl gave out a desperate and piteous whine of pain. Her back and legs were covered with welts. She was so terrified that her mind had ceased to work and she ran screaming into her gag from spot to spot, the man inexorably trailing her. She collapsed on the ground and tried to roll herself into a little ball, to deny the reality of the pain and the whip. But the man just stood there, rhythmically laying the whip on her again and again. Her whole body revolted after each stinging kiss of the whip. She was crying, screaming inside. After the fourth excruciating blow, her mind forced her up to her feet again to run away, anywhere to avoid the whip.

Three more times, the naked, terrified ponygirl made the circuit of the ring, fleeing the inevitable. The man was quick and agile and responded quickly to her every move, striking her viciously again and again. Finally, as she cowered terrified against the paddock's corrugated steel wall, the man stopped. Jackie looked at him uncertainly. The face of her hood was soaked with her tears. Her back, legs and arms burned with the wounds that she had suffered. Was he taking a rest? Was there more to come?

Irkut admired the deep breathing, trembling, black hooded pony. Now he would see how smart she was. He was standing on the other side of the paddock, directly under the long arm of the training machine. He could see the pony watching him warily as it caught its breath. He took the handle of the whip and pointed to a spot just in front of him. Although he couldn't see its face, he knew that the pony was going through an intense crisis. If she came to him, who knew what he would do? If she stayed away, he would probably keep whipping her anyway. But to voluntarily to put herself with arms length of her tormentor? That was something that was not easy to do. He pointed again to the spot in front of him. This time, the pony, after a few seconds, began to walk over to him warily. "She is smart," Irkut remarked to himself.

Jackie had gone through several calculations in her mind before surrendering to the brutal man's command.

He looked like he could whip her all day. She was tired and scared and oozing with pain. He had proven his mastery over her, for now at least. Whatever he had planned for her, she reasoned, it would be worse if she disobeyed him. She crept over to him slowly, keeping her eye on the long tassel of the whip. When she knew was inside the striking zone, she relaxed somewhat, knowing that he would have to step away from her to whip her again. The pony whip was only good at a distance and not intended for close in work.

When the pony had brought itself to the spot where he had pointed, Irkut stood and stared into its eyes for a few moments. He wanted it to see the cruelty lodged in his.

A shiver of fear ran through Jackie's body as she looked into the cold, hard eyes of her trainer. She could see that he would do anything he wanted to her, that her pain meant nothing but as an ally to his will. Her stomach fell and a wave of despair ran through her.

Irkut took the chain at the end of the long arm of the training machine and clipped it to a ring that was connected to the front of Jackie's gag. She had not seen it there and was surprised when her head was pulled upwards. Her vision was that of the sky above and nothing else. It was a clear day, something Jackie had not taken notice of until now. All she could see through the tiny holes in her hood was the heavy, wooden pole above her and the chain connecting her to it against a background of light blue. She heard the man's footsteps in the dirt as he walked away from her. She knew that he was planning something terrible for her and she whined and cried in fear. Why was this happening to her, she asked the open sky? How could she escape it? How long and how cruelly would this man torment her?

Irkut returned to where Jackie stood on her tip toes. She heard him pounding something into the ground behind her. It was a long, steel spike with a short chain attached to one end. When he had sunk it into the ground so that only the chain was showing, he took the chain, looped it through rings on the back of Jackie's boots and connected it to itself. The effect was to pull Jackie's feet closely together and to immobilize them.

Jackie felt her feet confined. When the man walked away, she tried to move them but found that they were tightly bound. Panic arose in her as she realized that she was absolutely at the man's mercy. Her fear was justified when she heard the 'swoosh' of the rattan cane through the air behind her.

"Oh, god, no!" she cried out in her mind. He was going to beat her again! She did not understand it. She had done nothing wrong, not since the escape attempt at the other place. And she had already been punished for that! Why was she being beaten now? She knew that she would not be able to stand being beaten again, that she would give anything, do anything, to prevent it. But she had no power to speak, nothing to bargain with. Whatever this man wanted, he could just take. But if that was so, why was she to be whipped?

Irkut heard the pony making little whinnying sounds behind her gag. She was pulling at the bindings to her wrists, desperately trying to free them. He had purposely swung the cane through the air so that she would know what was coming and to increase her apprehension. She yanked at the chains holding her in place. The wooden spar to which her gag was attached was strong and unyielding. Given an hour or two, she might actually be able to work the chain at her feet free of the earth, but she did not have that long.

The pony trainer knew all about her escapade at Khalid's He knew that she needed to be taught fully and firmly her place. This would be a special beating, one she would never forget.

The first blow of the cane struck across the front of Jackie's close confined thighs. It burned like fire when it hit and Jackie screamed in pain and fear. The next blow came a few seconds later across her breasts. The pain went straight to her brain. She had never imagined her beautiful breasts as being such a source of pain to her. The next blow came across her belly, leaving a long trail of red behind. Irkut needed to be careful there for tomorrow the new pony would be given her markings and if he wounded her too severely the tattoo of the angry black head of the mastiff would have to be postponed for a few days. So he concentrated on other parts of her body.

He laid strokes across her upper back, across the backs of her thighs, and especially hard ones on the well padded rear cheeks. The ponygirl tried to twist and turn away from the blows, but she was held fast. She cried and mewed and made just about every sound a gagged, tormented, former woman could make. She screamed intently when he laid several blows directly on her confined hands. It was an area much ignored by other trainers, but Irkut knew how sensitive the hands and fingers were.

He had decided to give her twenty five strokes. He walked around her leisurely, at a steady pace, striking out at her flesh in a regular cadence. Each blow came exactly five seconds after the last. It was all over in a little less than two minutes. But it was the longest two minutes of Jackie's life. She could not see him, but her ears followed the man as he walked around her. After the fifth or sixth blow, she had caught on to the pattern and knew when the next blow was coming. But no matter how much she steeled herself for it, she still cried and screamed when it bit her flesh.

Her whole body seemed a terrible, screaming wound. The poor ponygirl was worked up into a frenzy of pain.

While she screamed and moaned and tried to beg for mercy, Irkut coolly and calmly applied the prescribed strokes while taking in appreciatively the shaking and writhing of her beautiful body.

When done, Irkut put away the cane. He came back to the sobbing pony which was held up only by the chain connected to her gag. Her legs were useless, being turned all to jelly by the beating. She jumped when Irkut placed his hand on her tortured rump. He noticed that the bright red traces of the cane's kiss melded well with the pony's dark brown skin. He stood behind her and, reaching around her body, took her lustfully plump breasts in his hands. He pressed his body against hers. She was a desirable ponygirl. The men were going to line up to fuck her. In a few weeks, she would begin to actually look forward to her assaults as she was brought to orgasm again and again. It would be her only respite from terror and tedium. For when she was not being beaten or driven to physical extremes while training, she would be bound and locked into her stall in the pony barn, unable to move, alone, with only the bare, wooden wall in front of her to look at.

Now, he would take his pleasure with the animal. He disconnected the boots from the chain in the ground and then walked in front of her and unhooked her gag from the wooden spar. The disheartened pony sank to her knees. Irkut withdrew his cock from his pants. It was turgid with anticipation. The expressionless head of the pony looked at it and then up at Irkut's face. Irkut could not see whether she registered resignation or dismay at what she was going to be required to do. But there were very few other interpretations of Irkut's action in exposing his fleshy weapon and so he was sure that she knew what would be required of her.

Actually, it was both resignation and dismay, interlaced with a good deal of anger. This man had cruelly abused her, and had not so much as spoken a word to her. And now, she was to pleasure him. She had not minded his hands on her breasts. They were cool compared to the hot, abused flesh. But this? Was she supposed to meekly accept his cock in her mouth?

Ultimately, like all but a very few of the ponygirls, Jackie decided that she would cooperate in her own debasement. At this stage, most of the ponygirls still did not know that there was literally no chance of an escape or deliverance from their new role in life. To refuse to cooperate, or to do damage to the tender man flesh exposed to her teeth and jaws would bring severe and painful punishment, maybe even death. Maybe they would cut out her tongue and pull out all her teeth. They could bake her over a low fire for hours and hours until she was dead. They could do anything they wanted and then all chances of escape would be lost. No, it was better to submit, to comply.

Irkut removed the thick gag from Jackie's mouth and presented his stiffening cock to the ponygirl's pursed lips. She allowed the thick rod to pass over them and accepted the fat head into her mouth. Jackie had sucked a thousand cocks. But she had never felt so degraded and abased as she did right now. This man was her torturer. His hot meat was like an evil snake that had entered her mouth. Her stomach turned as she pressed her lips against it and caressed it with her tongue. Even when that pimp had made her suck off all of his friends, just before Jake put the guy away, she had not felt revolted at this usually pleasant act. Jackie liked the taste of a man's cock, the sweat, the smell of his loins. She liked the hardness and the passion she could arouse. But this was different. This act was to put an accent on the lesson that she had just learned, that she was a helpless prisoner subject to the whims and desires of others, a creature bent to their wills.

Irkut sighed as his cock sank into the pony's suppliant mouth. He noted her skillful use of her tongue, the quality of her technique. Of course, he was aware of the small chance that the pony might, as an act of irrational rebellion, decide to punish the vulnerable tool of the man who had caused her so much pain, but he was ready for it. At the slightest hint that she was going to bite him, he would strike viciously at her temple with his fist. Her lights would go out and her jaw would slacken. He had had to do it once. Afterwards, he spent three days torturing the pony until he was satisfied that it would never do it again.

Waves of pleasure flowed over Irkut as Jackie's ardent mouth and lips brought their warmth and softness to his hard cock. After the first few minutes, he was able to allow himself to relax, confident that the ponygirl was submissively accepting her task. He put his hands on the black shrouded head and guided it to the rhythm that he sought. He moaned as his juices began to rise.

Jackie felt and heard the man's lust getting ready to go on the boil. She had a whore's skill in bringing a man to climax. But the thought of this man's spunk defiling her made her heart pound and her stomach turn. She gave a little squeal of dismay when she felt the prick begin to throb. Her hands twisted behind her and her knees pressed hard into the bare earth beneath her. The man's hand had grabbed her ponytail and held her face tightly against his stomach as he orgasmed. He moaned and his body wavered as the force of his pleasure made his knees weak. This was the time to strike, Jackie thought. But what if what Jake had told her was true? What if she was really going to get a million dollars when all of this was done and through? She had just suffered an excruciatingly painful beating and had no doubt that she would receive more.

But, if she could hack it, survive, endure, she would be rich. She would never have to take any man's cock that she didn't want again.

As the cock throbbed and pulsed in her mouth, its head poking past the edge of her throat, Jackie resigned herself to her fate.

CHAPTER NINE
LIGHTNING'S SUMMER VACATION

Lightning, the former Maddy Burnham, sensed that she had entered an entirely new phase in her existence as a ponygirl. Gone were the days of intense training she had undergone in the spring. The daily violence she had experienced as a yearling and during the racing season was now reduced to only an occasional, seemingly random event. The days were long and leisurely. Even the many tedious hours that she spent standing in her stall in the pony barn, her ankles forced far apart, her vision limited to the bare wall in front of her, seemed less oppressive.

Her days began always the same, the morning shave and cleansing, a delicious orgasm, breakfast and the daily footrace. Each morning, all the racing ponygirls were assembled at the track and made to take a lap around it. The one that finished last received a beating while tied over a rail and then the carnal abuse of whatever trainer or groom inclined to use her. In the beginning of her life as a ponygirl, Lightning had finished last almost every day. She had suffered cruelly both while bent over the rail and at the hands of her trainer, who punished her essentially for being punished. But she had learned to run with all her heart and soul and these days it seemed almost leisurely to trot around the track and, if not finishing first, at least finishing near the lead.

The fact that she was aware that there were ponygirls younger than her at the estate somehow gave her a feeling of accomplishment. What they were learning, she already knew. Although she did feel sorry for a slender, orange tailed yearling that seemed to finish last every day.

Lightning could hear her moan and sob each time as she was led to the rail for her punishment.

After the informal, daily race, she would spend some time in her stall, legs fixed spread apart, her nose ring connected to the wall in front of her by a chain. At those times, she would try and empty her mind and just let the sensuousness of her now extremely fit and ever naked, hardened body course through her. She would focus on that morning's orgasm, whether she had been given the benefit of her groom's fat cock or not, how intense had been the throes of pleasure. She would recall the thrill of her victories during the racing season, the pleasant flesh of her temporary racing partner Persephone. And she would listen to the quiet cacophony of the pony barn, the tread of the men's boots, the rustle of chains in the other stalls, the moans of a pony being serviced by one of the broad shouldered, young grooms.

And yet, her pervasive unhappiness at her fate would creep in as she stood there so motionless, so cruelly confined for an hour or two, sometimes more. Her body was her prison. The men had captured it, made it their own, forced her to occupy it and activate it for them at their commands. When the feeling of despair and self pity would creep into her, she would fight it, hold back her tears. What was the use? It was better to stop thinking of the past, thinking of herself as a woman, even a former one. She would breathe deeply, close her eyes, numb herself. It was the only thing she could do.

Not every day, but frequently, a groom or trainer would stop by her stall and, after stroking her thighs and breasts, mount her from behind, bringing her to crisis easily, pumping his hot spewm deeply into her womb or her bowels. She would not see the face of her benefactor, her head firmly fixed in place. Sometimes she would try and guess who it was. Glad at the interruption of her deadly boredom, she would often recognize the deep, guttural groans or the rough, forceful hands. They might whisper her name as they plumbed her depths, sighing the name, 'Molnya', as their passion overtook them.

Around mid-morning, one of the grooms would take her out and harness her to a carriage. Sometimes she would be placed in the traces alongside one of the other ponies, and sometimes she would be harnessed to the sulky carriage to run by herself. These were really just leisurely runs, to keep the ponies in trim. But Lightning would enjoy the workouts, the coursing of her blood through her veins, the deep, heavy breaths, the tension on the muscles of her legs and shoulders, even the feel of the heavy carriage behind her. She liked it most when she ran alone, because she could just let herself go without minding the pace of the other pony.

After her morning run, she would be hosed off and washed with a large, soft, soapy sponge. The coolness of the water was refreshing and the tactile sensation of the sponge covering her breasts and thighs made her lustful. It was not unusual for one of the grooms or trainers, attracted by the tableau of the handling of her flesh, to take her aside and bring her to her knees, either to fuck her doggy style in the freshly mowed grass, or to have her give him oral service. Lightning enjoyed the feel of the hard, warm flesh in her mouth and would take her time caressing his manhood, running her soft lips down its length, tickling its undersides with her tongue.

Some of the men used her roughly, wanting only the feel of her throat around their cocks and would take hold of her long, auburn tail and force her head down against their bellies. Even then, Lightning would revel in the liberation of her mouth from her gag or bit and open herself so that the fat heads of their pricks rested in her esophagus. She would shiver with pleasure when the tube of hard meat began to pulse and throb inside her.

After her shower, she would be allowed to join the other ponies in a large, grassy field, surrounded by large, white rail fences, to lie in the grass or to commune with her sister ponies.

The field was actually more like a glade. It sloped down from the area next to the pony barn to a cool stream and a stand of tall oak trees. There was a pond and some sitting stones alongside it. Lightning often spent her entire morning in anticipation of her time in the pasture. It was a truly bucolic setting with wildflowers, birds singing, squirrels and even field mice. Lightning would watch one or another of the estate's many cats hunting like some fierce tiger, crawling along, crouched in the grass, or waiting silently and patiently for its prey to enter the zone of danger. Lightning would watch the drama between prey and predator closely, praying each time for the mouse to escape, crying softly inside when the cat proved supreme and walked away with the squealing little creature in its jaw.

The first time Lightning had been released into the pasture she was overcome with an immense sense of liberation. There were no trainers or grooms, no men at all. The other blue hooded ponies were gathered down by the pond, some of them splashing water on each other playfully, others lying stretched out in the shade, reveling in their relative freedom. When she saw Persephone, her heart leapt. Persephone had been her cart mate when she ran as a yearling in the beginning of racing season. Their driver, a wiry, blond haired and bearded man had been kind and loving to the pair and allowed them to spend off hours nestled against each other's flesh, or even, after removing their gags or bits, permitted them to kiss and caress each other with their lips.

But Lightning had not been able to spend any time with Persephone after she had been selected to replace an injured pony in the one pony sulky. That trainer, a four foot tall dwarf with an angry mien and a scarred face, had been inordinately cruel and harsh to her. Although his technique had shown dividends when she won the 1500 meter sulky championship, it had been a hard, terror filled time for Lightning. And she had missed the pony who had become her lover.

Persephone had seen Lightning at about the same time. The ponies squealed with glee and ran up against one another. It was the practice to send the ponies into the field wearing their racing bits and Lightning was able to rub her lips against Persephone's and utter mewing sounds of happiness.

Persephone was a blond tailed pony and had large, pleasing breasts. She was shorter and stockier than Lightning, but was a hardworking pony and had developed both speed and endurance while matched with her. Lightning and Persephone had won nearly all their races and had been the favorites to win the yearling trophy. She didn't know how Persephone had made out after they had been separated. She had seen her paired with a tall, lanky, brown haired pony and seen them training together. But she never saw them race and, of course, no one ever bothered to tell her how they made out in the Spring Tournament. This was not unusual, because ponygirls, not being considered human, were never told anything.

Lightning wore the gold medal signifying her victory in the finals on her collar and she was happy to see a silver medal on Persephone's. She assumed, correctly, that Persephone and her mate had finished second in their division.

Lightning kissed and pushed her body up next to Persephone's. The other pony responded warmly.

Lightning had no idea of what was allowed and not allowed in the pasture, and she looked nervously back through the tiny holes in her hood at the pony barn to see if anyone was watching. Two men, she couldn't tell who, were leaning against the fence smoking, apparently enjoying the view of the ponies at play. She looked over and saw a small rise under the shade of a tall oak tree and motioned to it to Persephone with her head. The other pony nodded her understanding and they trotted over there excitedly.

Lightning knelt in the soft grass and Persephone knelt down in front of her. They pushed their bodies close until their breasts were pressed hard against the other's and rubbed their lips together. Lightning yearned to push her tongue into her lover's mouth, but it was locked in place by a steel plate connected to the bit. There was pleasure, though, in the contact of their lips and the warmth of each other's body.

Persephone, of course, wore the same featureless, tight fitting, blue hood that Lightning wore and she had never seen the other pony's face. The shape of her body and breasts, though, were unmistakable and the Cyrillic letters across her chest were easily recognizable. Lightning had never spoken a word to her and knew nothing about her. But she felt that she knew her inwardly, having gone through the travails of training and racing together. Her flesh tingled at the points of their contact, their soft, plump breasts, the fronts of their sculpted thighs.

They fell together to the ground and lay on their sides, pressing their bodies as closely together as they could. Lightning was hungry for the taste of the other's flesh and, after pushing her to her back, drew her hot lips down over Persephone's tattooed chest and took a nipple of her breast between her lips. The bit prevented her from bringing it wholly within her mouth, but she was able to grip it softly and then rub her lips across Persephone's areola until she felt the nipple grow stiff. She shifted to the other breast and was rewarded by a sensuous moan from her lover.

Slowly, Lightning brought her lips down Persephone's taut belly and over the yellow, tattooed, angry wolf that they both shared there. As she neared the crux of Persephone's thighs, the pony spread her legs widely, as if yearning for her cart mate's kiss on her nether lips.

Lightning took her time in pleasuring the slit between Persephone's legs. She savored the aroma of her desire and the taste of her fluids on her lips. She heard Persephone begin to whine and struggle underneath her and she looked up at her lover. Persephone was pushing her head to the side and twisting her torso. Her meaning was immediately evident to Lightning and, the pony readily complied with the other pony's wishes. She turned her body around and lifted her leg so that she was straddling Persephone's chest. She spread her knees apart and lowered her head again to her partner's moist, dilated pussy. As she did so, she felt the other pony's lips brush against her own sex and a wave of pleasure and happiness ran through her.

The two ponies ground their mouths against each other's sexes. The warmth of their bodies against each other's was pure ecstasy. Lightning's mind was in heaven as she supped at Persephone's lush pussy and felt the lips of the other's tease her hardened clit. Lightning's passion began to rise and when she felt the tell tale signs of her impending orgasm, she began to cry with joy. Her body tensed and quaked as the pulses of pleasure ran through her. She felt her lover's body tense as well and heard the pony crying out in pleasure beneath her.

When the mind befogging pulses of their orgasms faded, they rolled over as one and repeated their lustful oral caresses again, this time with Persephone on top. Lightning's second orgasm was more powerful than her first and she cried out, "Oooooooompf! Oooooooompf! Oooooooompf!" as each intense contraction of her womb drove all other sensations or thoughts from her mind.

Afterwards, the ponies lay with their bodies intertwined, lying dreamily in the shade of the big tree. After a while, Lightning noticed that another pony had joined them. It was Persephone's tall partner, a former, young, Australian girl from near Brisbane. Lightning couldn't see her face, but she sensed sadness in the pony as she sat cross legged a little away from the lovers. Lightning felt sorry for the pony and got up and knelt next to her, rubbing her head against hers. Persephone rose as well and the two ponies pushed the Australian to her back and brought her to pleasure jointly. The three of them lay quietly, nestled together until they heard the ringing of a bell and saw the other ponies moving back towards the pony barn.

During the eight weeks or so that were considered ponygirl summer, each morning, and each afternoon, except when it rained, after the training runs had been completed, the ponies were allowed to relax and enjoy each other in the pasture. It was a fairly universal custom to allow the ponies this recreation. No mind could stand the ever present stress and strain of confinement and abuse that ponygirls were subject to without some form of release. It stroked whatever conscience the masters had at depriving these former human females of their personhoods to watch them frolic and play together.

It was from this that the myth of the content, happy, ponygirl derived. When guests and, yes, sometimes tourists, came by the estates to see the ponygirls at work and play, this is often what they saw. Through binoculars, they could watch the ponies making love, cuddling together, splashing and running in the stream. It seemed utterly idyllic. If one didn't know better, and few outside the sport had any real idea of the extremes of punishment and abuse that the ponies often suffered, one would think that the former women had been given a gift of the return to childhood, a species of Eden. But then, they hadn't watched while a pony was reduced to a blubbering mass through the use of a whip, watched while a new pony struggled as it was repeatedly raped by its new masters or listened at night to the sobs and cries of the newly tattooed and pierced ponygirl, alone and bound in her stall, trying to fathom the reality of what was happening to her.

It was after a little more than two weeks of this relatively tranquil existence that Drabik finally returned to the estate. First, he had to endure the ceremonial welcome back of Grobgy, a man who he was growing to resent and hate for his relative indolence, and then there was the obligatory evening at the inn with Grobgy's oversexed and beautiful daughter, Anya. It was obligatory, but sensually rewarding nonetheless. He had tied her up during one of their trysts and since then he had used some form of bondage on her every time that they made love.

He had begun to attire her in some of the accessories of a pony girl. This time, in addition to the ponygirl collar and gag, he added the heavy ponygirl boots to their costume drama. Anya swooned when he put them on her and she sucked his cock for twenty five minutes, on her knees, her hands bound behind her. After he came the first time, and spilled his seed down her throat, he made her keep his softened cock in her mouth until he was hard again. The second time, he splashed his come all over her face. Later, bound to the bed, her legs splayed widely, she screamed in pleasure into her gag as he tongued her pussy.

The next morning, he had determined to play his little Lightning a visit. She had been on his mind almost constantly and part of his resentment at Grobgy was the fact that he had sent him on his lethal journey the night after the championship banquet, interfering with his plans of a private 'welcome home' party with the ponygirl champion. He had resented it last spring when she had been taken from his supervision and turned over to a driver, even though he knew that this was what would happen and the fact that he had trained at least forty other ponygirls without so much as a qualm.

Somehow, this pony had bewitched him. He yearned for her flesh, the caress of her mouth. He burned to have the touch of her flesh in his hands, to enter her and have his pleasure with her. Anya had sensed this and he was careful not to let her know the extent of his obsession. He knew that he needed to hide his passion for the ponygirl or she would face the spoiled rich woman's vindictive side. Today, he was determined to break the spell the ponygirl had over him once and for all.

Lightning was in the pony barn awaiting her morning jaunt when he entered her stall. Ponygirls were not assigned to particular stalls. That would be too much like awarding them property rights. It was better that their environment shift, that they be reminded of their lack of human status. When a pony was placed in a stall, any available stall, a small plate with its name engraved on it was placed on a hook attached to a tall board over which was the number of the stall. Drabik had to check the board before locating her.

His fires began to rise immediately upon viewing her naked, exposed flesh. He rubbed his rough hands over her flanks and cupped her breasts from behind. Leaning himself against her, he reached for her head and lowered the flaps on her hood so that her eyes were covered. He wanted this to be a surprise.

Lightning was surprised when her eyes were darkened. This had not happened during the day for quite a while and it usually bode no good. She felt her ankles released and then the chain that linked her golden nose ring to the wall.

A leash was affixed to her collar and she followed docilely as she was led through the barn.

Drabik took the disturbed pony to a gallows like post far away from the main training area. He wanted relative privacy for what he was going to do. Not that anyone would interfere or criticize him. That was what ponygirls were for, when they were not racing. But he wanted to enjoy this alone.

When they reached the post, Drabik released the leash from the pony's collar and attached a heavy leather harness around her upper torso. The post was like an inverted 'L' and a chain dangled from the horizontal beam. It attached to a hook in the top of the harness. Drabik pulled it tight until the ponygirl was on the tips of her toes.

Lightning whined when she felt herself attached to the chain. She knew that she was about to be beaten. It had been more than a week since she had been brought out from her stall at night and thrashed and she had hoped that she would be free from bodily harm for a while. She started to sweat as she anticipated her abuse. Why and by whom she was being tortured, she didn't know. It didn't really matter. There was no real sense of deserving to any of the torture that she had suffered, although when she disappointed her masters or broke some rule, she at least knew why she was being thrashed. But any question of fairness was ridiculous when taken in light of the reduction of the blameless female to bestial status to begin with. All of the ponies had been innocent, or relatively so, young women before they had been torn from their homes, tattooed and shackled, raped and whipped. Under these circumstances, deserving was an absurd concept.

Drabik hooked the pony's boots together and stood back from her. He could see her trembling as she stood there, her fine breasts tremoring slightly, the glistening of sweat on her chest. He stepped up to her again and caressed her breasts gently. He had missed them. He ran his thumbs over the nipples until they were stiff. The place he had selected was quiet. It was on the far side of the practice track and he could hear the occasional spinning wheels of a carriage and the tramp of ponygirl boots in the dirt as they passed. There was a copse of woods nearby and the sounds of birds chirping and singing rose from it. Lightning heard these sounds too, concentrating on them, trying to drive from her mind the consciousness of what was about to happen to her. She had been beaten before. She would be beaten again. She would live through it. But the prospect of being mercilessly thrashed still filled her with anguish.

Drabik had brought an assortment of whips with him in a little leather case not unlike a golf bag. He placed it down and selected his first instrument. The first thing that he wanted to do was to make the pony's skin raw and irritated. He pulled out a flogger, a short handled whip with flat, thin tassels. It would bruise the skin everywhere it landed. He decided to start with the breasts.

Drabik brought his right arm back and dashed the hard, thick, flat tassels against the pony's soft, full mounds. She stiffened and screamed her pain into her gag. Drabik counted to ten, letting the burning sensation of the last blow fade and struck again, this time across the taut belly, across the yellow tattoo of the angry, rampant wolf. Lightning moaned and cried, her body jerking and contorting. Next he struck the thighs, and then the breasts again and then the belly. He walked around her and belabored her hard, voluptuous rear cheeks, the back of her legs and thighs. Lightning's voice was a constant moan. She hopped on her bound feet, desperate to avoid the blows. She was able to twist and turn, but it made no matter, since Drabik could walk silently around her, unseen, and strike at any body part at will.

He continued his assault until Lightning's body was a coat of red. She looked like she had been in the sun too long, something not likely since all of the ponies wore strong sun block while outside. He allowed the pony some respite. He lit a cigarette and watched her sway back and forth on her chain, moaning lowly. She was a beautiful creature and he enjoyed tormenting her. He thought briefly about his need to destroy beauty, of the pretty, little Russian girl he had turned over to Mikhail, the many ponies he had trained. But, when he tossed his cigarette onto the ground, he pushed those thoughts away.

Next was the long, thin lash. It would leave a thin line of angry red wherever it landed and, if he struck hard enough, a seeping trail of blood. He didn't want to cut her up, and so he would measure his blows carefully. His goal was pain and not damage.

As before, his first target was the pony's pretty breasts. They were a pinkish color now and when the lash landed, it struck already painfully abused skin.

"Oooooeeeeeooooo!" the pony called out through the thick, leather plug in its mouth. It was like someone had dragged a piece of barbed wire across her breasts. She shook her faceless, expressionless, blue clad head back and forth wildly as she cried out forlornly for pity. But her words weren't heard, only a high pitched screech. Drabik filled Lightning's body with bright red lines. Across her belly, her thighs, her back, her arms and legs.

Through her torment, Lightning came to understand who her torturer was. Only her former trainer could hold such hatred for her to put her through this slow, deliberate, prolonged hell. She thought back to the hands on her breast, the smell of his cigarette, the sound of his boots. It was him all right. Not that knowledge of that did her any good. She cried and danced and swung her body to and fro nonetheless.

Drabik's shirt was drenched with sweat when he finished. He looked upon his handiwork with satisfaction. The fine, young body of the ponygirl was awash with long, red stripes. She hung in her harness, moaning dismally. But he had not yet had enough. He went back to his bag and drew out the heavy, leather handled, oaken dowel. He approached the sobbing creature and struck out savagely, driving the heavy club against Lightning's right thigh. It landed with a dull thud and elicited a mournful, low moan from the pony. He struck her left thigh, her arms and the backs of her legs. And then he was done.

Lightning sagged in the leather harness. She had no more energy to moan or cry out. Her head drooped and her boots dragged on the ground. She was conscious of only her misery. She hardly felt it when her harness was lowered from the gibbet, barely noticed when she was pressed to her knees and her gag removed. Were it not for the length of chain that connected her harness to the wooden post above her, Lightning would have fallen to the ground.

Drabik's lust was blinding. He cared not that the pony was barely conscious, he drove his hardened cock into her mouth and found the narrowness of her throat. He grabbed her reddish brown colored ponytail and used it to force her head back and forth over his throbbing prick. It only took a few strokes and his jism was shooting down her throat. The pony gagged and sputtered as she tried to accommodate the copious flow.

Physically sated, the harsh, implacably cruel ponygirl trainer stepped back from the coughing pony. To his dismay, the darkness that had covered his heart was still there. He had hoped to expiate it through his fiendish assault on the body of its source. Rage filled him. Leaving his benumbed victim behind, he stomped off, his fists clenched tightly in self hatred.

Later, one of the grooms came upon Lightning. They had been looking for her and were afraid that somehow she had escaped. He looked on her tortured form aghast. Beating a pony was one thing, but torturing her to unconsciousness, disabling her, that was another.

He ran back to the pony barn and recruited two of the dray ponies and a flat cart and drove it to where Lightning knelt in the dust. He picked her up and gently laid her on the cart, carefully returning her gag to her mouth. He drove the cart back to the pony barn and, with the help of another groom, brought the injured pony inside. They laid her on a training table and washed her body clean of sweat and blood. Lightning recoiled when she awoke to find strong, rough hands on her body, but soon felt relief as cool, wet cloths were used to sooth her wounds. The groom noted the incipient black and blue marks on her legs and arms and had another groom ice them down while he applied a healing ointment to the long, angry, red stripes. Someone poured a glass of vodka and the groom gave it to the pony to drink. Afterwards, she was taken to a stall and allowed to rest, bound to the floor.

Drabik had returned to his small cabin on the outskirts of the estate. He roomed alone, unlike all of the other trainers who doubled up in rooms at the bunkhouse. He was permanently assigned a slave girl, who was rotated every few days, and a tiny, cowering, naked girl, kneeling in the center of the three room cabin, greeted him as he angrily slammed the door against the wall as he entered. He slammed the door shut behind him and proceeded to toss the small kitchen table into the air, throw a chair against the wall and swipe a counter full of dishes and glasses onto the floor.

The slave girl, who had heard of the cruelty of the 'dark master' as he was known among the slave girls, cowered in the corner, fearful for her life. Drabik saw her and, grabbing her by the hair, dragged her into the bedroom and flung her on the bed. He tore off his clothes and, making the girl kneel down before him, pushed his still hard cock against her rear opening. The slave girl, a diminutive, blond haired, Danish girl called Rena, cried with pain as her rear passage was torn by the man's brutal thrusts. Pounding her mercilessly, Drabik groaned loudly when he came. His thick, rigid pole throbbed inside the poor girl and filled her bowels with his seed.

When he was done, he collapsed on top of her. All of his energy was gone. His lust was sated, although his brain still burned.

The slave girl knelt still, shivering with fear under the brutal man. Her tiny, little girl breasts were crushed against her knees and her face pressed down hard on the mattress. She dared not move, although the heavy body of the taller, stronger man was crushing the breath from her. She had never seen such rage in all her days and prayed that he would be becalmed when he awoke.

Luckily for her, Drabik soon came back to awareness. He rolled off of the girl and lay back next to her. He could feel her trembling next to him and, angrily pushed her off of the bed. She fell to the floor in a clatter of arms and legs and gave a little, frightened cry. This angered Drabik all the more and he got up from the bed and dragged her to her feet. He locked her leather bracelets together behind her and slapped her across the face. She cried out at the blow and fell back to the floor. Drabik took her by the arm and bought her back to her feet. His hand was poised for another blow when he came to his senses. He had wreaked enough violence for one day. He dragged her by the arm from the bedroom, opened the door to his cabin and threw her out onto the grass outside, slamming the door shut behind her. Grabbing a bottle of vodka, he went back to the bedroom.

The little, Danish, slave girl didn't know what to do. She didn't want to face the cruel 'dark master' again, but was afraid to go back to the main house lest she be punished for leaving her duty station. Tearful, the mark of Drabik's hand on her cheek, she crawled up onto the small porch of the cabin and knelt by the door. She was still there, late the next morning, cowering and naked, her bound arms behind her, when Drabik awoke from his drunken stupor.

* * * * * * * * * * * * *

When Grobgy heard how Drabik had so callously abused and tortured his best ponygirl, he was beside himself with rage. Twice, he had begun to walk down to Drabik's cabin, his 9mm Makorov strapped to his hip. Grobgy still favored the semiautomatic pistol of his police days and was a deadly shot with it. It would have been an interesting confrontation. But each time, he retreated to the mansion. He cursed and swore, angered by his apparent need to choose between his best killer and his favorite pony. The house full of slave girls all ran for cover each time they saw him storming back to the house. Finally, he determined to let himself cool off before making his decision.

In the morning, he decided to pay a visit to the pony barn. He found Lightning still in her stall, bound in her sleeping position. He closed the stall door behind him and began to undo her ankle and leg bindings. The pony began to shiver and shake. When he disconnected her neck chain, she began to whine and cry. He lifted her to her feet and pulled back the Velcro tabs that blocked her vision.

Lightning was sure that her trainer had come back to beat her again. When she saw the swarthy face of her owner, his tell tale thick, black moustache, the piercing blue eyes, she was confused. What did he want with her?

Was he going to torment her as well? Unconsciously, she shied away from him, but the weakness in her thigh muscles caused her to collapse.

Grobgy caught her as she fell and lowered her to the floor. He could tell that she was crying and her body was shivering with fear. He stroked her hooded head gently and spoke soft words of endearment to her in his deep, sonorous voice. It took some time, but he was finally able to becalm the terrorized pony. He loosened her gag and took a small piece of sugar from his pocket and fed it to her.

The diet of a ponygirl was nourishing, but notoriously bland. What mattered fine tastes and spices to an animal? And so Lightning's mouth experienced an explosion of sensation as the cube began to melt on her tongue. The long denied experience was soothing to the former woman. In spite of her fear, her continuing pain, she managed a small smile.

Grobgy was pleased. Perhaps all was not lost after all. He had seen ponygirls whose spirit had been broken. They became useless as racers, and not good for much else. This pony would need a good deal of nurturing to bring her back to usefulness.

For the rest of the morning, Grobgy sat in the pony stall with Lightning, holding her in his lap, singing Russian lullabies and rocking her back and forth. He caressed her breasts and kissed them tenderly. He lay her down and gently massaged her abused muscles. When the groom came to apply her ointment for her wounds, he took it from him and applied it himself. When the lunchtime meal came, he crushed more sugar cubes into it and convinced the pony to eat.

When she was done, he took the blue hooded, faceless pony back into his lap. He had her sit with her back to him, with her legs spread wide. Humming lowly to her, he reached up and closed her eye flaps, rendering her back into darkness.

Lightning found the comforts of her owner soothing. She knew that she should curse him, that she should have spit out his sweets, dared him to murder her. For as she had lain bound in her cell overnight, she had yearned for the comfort of death. It didn't matter how it came, how painful it was, as long as the end result was deliverance from this hellish life. But the soothing voice of the huge man who owned her, his rough but gentle hands, soon had her mesmerized. She allowed herself to drift off into a more peaceful place, to let her recent trauma wash away.

When the pony was nestled in his lap, her head back, resting on his strong shoulder, Grobgy took his large hands and placed them under her ample breasts cupping them. At first, he just held them, letting his heat pass into them. Then, after about fifteen minutes, almost imperceptibly, he let his strong hands press the flesh gently, massaging the firm but soft orbs. Slowly, he moved his forefingers and thumbs to her nipples and pinched them mildly, pulling them out slightly from their base, stiffening them.

Lightning's mind reveled in the soothing touch of her master's hands. Her long, broad shouldered body seemed small, even childlike, when compared to the huge hulk of her owner. Gradually, she began to feel the familiar tingle of arousal in her loins. She sighed as the pleasurable sensations ran through her.

The terror of the Moscow and Kiev underworlds took note of the pony's acceptance of his caresses. He was careful not to rush things, and continued his loving ministrations to the pony's graceful mounds until he heard the pony moan with desire. Covering the right breast with his left hand, he let his other slide softly and slowly over her taut belly, over the inside of her widespread thighs and back again. He teasingly drew his hand over her bare nether lips, barely touching them and then returned to pinch the soft, fat labia together tenderly. He resumed his singing to her, humming the tune of a childhood song, while he passed a thick finger just inside them, tracing the line of her long slit.

The ponygirl knew what the heartless man was doing. He was seducing her back to life. For months, she had been conditioned to enjoy the use of her body as the single source of diversion from her bizarre and cruel existence. He was showing her a reason to live. If there was anything that ponies had over women it was the freedom to let their lusts carry them away wherever, whenever and at whosever's hands. It was, ironically, a compelled freedom, one forced on them by practice and necessity. But since the expectation of love, friendship, respect, appreciation and devotion had been mercilessly driven from them, since there was no longer any social stigma to unbridled wantonness, they could give full force to their lusts, come without restraint, let their desires carry them away.

Grobgy felt the ponygirl shift on his lap. His rock hard cock was captured by the space between her rear cheeks and her movements gave him quite a stir. She would get his cock, but later. This was to be all about her.

When his thick finger made contact with the pony's bud of pleasure, her thighs widened and she pressed her hips up to meet it. Grobgy was toying with the nipple of her breast as he softly stroked the little nub, drawing slow circles around it and covering it with the moisture from her now dewy slit. Lightning's lust was rising and she began to rock her hips slowly in time with the movements of her owner's finger. "Ohhhhhhhhhhh!" she sighed as the pleasure began to build. Grobgy slipped his left hand from Lightning's hardening breast to her mouth, stifling her moans. Ponygirls were not permitted words and Lightning's ejaculation of pleasure had come discomfortingly close. He wanted her healed, mentally as well as physically, but he certainly didn't want to undo months of training.

Lightning felt the rough hand of her master encompass her exposed mouth. It was actually a relief since, in her passion, she might have broken the cardinal rule and suffered for it. But with her sounds suppressed, she could let herself go, allow her desires to flow freely, to accept the passion imposed on her without reservation or fear.

The criminal overlord continued his attentions to the pony's dripping cleft. With two fingers now, he probed the wet canal deeply, drawing his fingers northwards, towards her stiffened clit. He stroked her slowly, rhythmically, gently and Lightning's body began to twist and turn in passionate response. He took his fingers, which were covered with the ooze of Lightning's lust and slipped them down over her perineum while he lifted his knees, raising the ponygirl's legs. Her rear aperture became exposed to him and he slid the lubricated fingers deep inside. His heavy, thick thumb penetrated her excited pussy and he began to stroke her earnestly in both places at once.

The pony's body jerked upon being doubly pierced, and began to shudder with its impending crisis. Lightning moaned into the hand that crushed her mouth as her wave crested. "Oooooooompf! Ooooooooooompf! Ooooooo-ooompf!" she called out as her hips thrust themselves at the hand that pleasured her. When she came, her body jerked and spasmed. Her pussy throbbed with hard, fiercely pleasurable contractions.

Afterwards, Lightning lay in her owner's arms, the memories of her intense climax echoing through her mind. She was thankful that the man had restored her belief in passion, her need for sexual completion. Laying in the dark during the night, she had feared that she had lost all her desire for pleasure, that life would have no draw for her at all. Turning to her side and pulling her knees to her chin,

the ponygirl huddled in the huge man's lap. She started to
cry with relief and gratitude, but soon drifted off to a
somnolent state, comforted by the powerful arms and the
sweet, low voice of her master.

Grobgy, too, dozed off. He awoke when he felt the
body of the desirable, young ponygirl stirring. He carefully
slid her off of his lap and brought her to her knees in front
of him. There was a bottle of water next to them and he
picked it up and let the thirsty ponygirl drink. The action
of her jaw and the entrapment of the bottle's neck by her
plump lips reminded him of his own lustful needs. He put
down the bottle and, leaning back against the wall of the
stall, slowly drew down his pants zipper and released his
stirring manhood. Lightning heard the tell tale sound and
anticipated her master's want. The eye holes in her hood
were still closed, and she edged forwards on her knees and
lowered her blue clad head, hoping for guidance.

Taking the pony's featureless head in his hands, Grobgy
drew it to his waiting cock. It bumped against her lips and
she opened her mouth wide to receive it. As he pushed her
head down into his loins, the ponygirl tensed her lips
around his now hardened pole and let them slide down its
length until the fat head breeched the entrance to her
throat.

Slowly and lovingly, Lightning serviced Grobgy's thick
tool. She could not recall whether she had ever delighted
him so before. She knew that he had plowed her fore and
aft on more than one occasion, but she didn't remember
whether she had ever drawn her lips tightly around his
heavy manhood. It was like heaven to her. She wanted,
earnestly, to express her appreciation for the man's tender,
healing touch. She yearned to hear him sigh and moan
with pleasure as a result of her efforts. She could not
express her gratitude verbally, and her expressionless visage
could not convey anything of which she felt. And so her

lips and tongue were her only instruments of communication.

Each time that the faceless and armless, naked ponygirl let her lips descend Grobgy's thick, hard shaft and the head of his cocked probed the tight tube in her throat, the man let out a low, almost mournful groan. And each time she drew her head back until her lips circled the bulbous head just at its underside, and she danced her tongue along its plump surface, he sighed.

When his cock exploded, Lightning drank down every drop of his thick, white cum. She sucked on his cock's head, drawing the precious liquid into her mouth, allowing its salty, pungent flavor to linger on her tongue.

Lightning held the master's cock in her mouth until it had softened to a mere turgid state. She felt his hands lift her head from its task, open her eyes' Velcro panels and raise her chin so that she could see her owner's face. He was smiling at her and he patted her head tenderly as an expression of his approval. "Pretty, little Molnya," he purred at her in Russian. He reached for the wall of the ponygirl stall and recovered Lightning's gag from where he had placed it. He proffered it to her mouth and she opened her lips obediently so that he could slide it home. He rose to his knees and, circling his hands behind her head, buckled it closed.

The ponygirl was overwhelmed with the man's body heat and the smell of his sweat as her face was drawn into his chest. Her mouth was filled with the thick wad of leather and her lips were covered by the leather shield attached. Grobgy placed his heavy, rough hands on the pony's shoulders and gently pushed her body back until she was again lying on the floor of her stall, on her thin, cotton pallet. As she watched him from behind her hood, her eyes barely perceptible behind the tiny holes, he closed her legs and tightened belts around her thighs and ankles. He secured her ankles and collar to chains anchored in the floor. He ran his hands over her legs and breasts and then over her veiled face. He closed the Velcro tabs and returned the ponygirl to sightlessness. It had been a good morning's work.

* * * * * * * * * * * * * * * * *

That afternoon, Grobgy had the contrite assassin up to his mansion. They were on a veranda overlooking the vast field that ran contiguous to the south side of the building, sitting at one of a number of glass patio tables. There was a sun blocking umbrella open over their heads and a blue watered, Olympic sized pool next to them. Drabik drank a large tomato juice, Grobgy drank vodka. The assassin barely touched the delightful lunch and barely noticed the nubile, young, naked slave girls who rushed in and out of the house ferrying their lunch and drinks to them.

"Anton," Grobgy said, exasperated, "you're supposed to be a professional. What's gotten into you? If you want to destroy a female, pick one of the slave girls, not my most promising ponygirl!"

"Axmail, please, don't, I acknowledge my error," Drabik replied. "I'll have nothing more to do with that pony. I,... I...." He paused, thinking of what he should tell his overlord and what he shouldn't. "Let's just say I made an error of judgment." Drabik's head was pounding, his throat was parched and there was weakness in his whole body. A quart and a half of 120 proof vodka in one night will do that to you.

"An error of judgment, yes," Grobgy responded. "But as to the rest, I don't agree. You have to make peace with this pony. Not today, that would be too soon, but in the next couple of days. I don't want this pony collapsing into a ball of jelly every time it sees you."

Drabik looked up at the hardened crime master. "I'm not going near her," Drabik said with a determined voice. "I have other work to do."

"You have other work to do," Grobgy insisted, "and that includes doing what I tell you. I don't care if you have to kiss her ass. I want that pony up and running as good as she was, and better, or I'll have your ass!"

A dark look passed across Drabik's face. This former sergeant of State Security was telling him to kiss a ponygirl's ass. He probably meant it literally. He prepared a harsh, bold answer, but then reason got the better of him. He was not ready to make a move on Axmail Grobgy. Things had to be put in place, certain loyalties won over, approval granted in higher places. He would bide his time and, for now, eat crow. "As you order it, sir," he answered. "Now may I go? My head is as big as a house."

Grobgy laughed. "I've been there. Go, with my blessing. Take one of the new girls with you for comfort."

As he watched Drabik go, Grobgy made a special note to have him watched. He needed to know whether he was nursing a viper in his bosom.

CHAPTER TEN
JACKIE LEARNS THE ROPES

The honeymoon was over on the second day. After her beating on the first day, while sucking her trainer's prick, Jackie had determined that she would be an obedient little ponygirl and go with the program. She had visions of a million dollar bills strewn all over her apartment and jumping into it, naked, for a swim. But, after letting the ponygirl eat some bland porridge from a bowl, and letting her pee, Irkut had strapped her into the training machine and practically driven her into the ground. Jackie had never worked so hard, even when training for varsity track in high school. Round and round the training paddock she ran, her gag ring attached to the overhead spar, her hands locked behind her. Slow and then fast, fast and then slow, the running went on seemingly for hours. Irkut encouraged her with the use of a quirt which he landed on her backside whenever she seemed to falter. When she fell, he was all over her with the leather weapon.

The new ponygirl was too tired to object that night when she was mounted in her stall and a steady stream of trainers and grooms came in to avail themselves of the exotic new pony. In spite of her lack of energy, bent over her rail, she bucked and whinnied several times as she was brought to the extremes of delight. Even the use of her smaller aperture brought her unexpected pleasure. She was finally bedded down after a groom washed away the spunk left behind to stream down her brown thighs.

It was her first night as a ponygirl and the day's events came rushing through her brain like a freight train. It had been nothing like she had imagined that it would be when she was nestled in Jake's strong arms back in Chicago. It was nothing like anyone could imagine. Lying on the floor, her ankles and thighs bound tightly, enveloped by darkness, she tried to put her predicament in some perspective. She had to keep telling herself that it was temporary. Sure five months was a long time, but it was not forever. She would fight to retain her sanity in these surreal circumstances.

She wondered what it would be like if she had had no inkling of what her fate would be when they first shaved and hooded her. Somehow the terror that she had felt at being handled was both made worse and attenuated by her foreknowledge. She had known that she would be treated just like an animal, Jake had told her so, but when that actually happened, everything inside her revolted against it. On the long ride in the back of the pony van, she had been in constant dread of the rough treatment that she knew she would have to soon begin to endure. And so it kind of balanced out. But knowing what dreadful events the future held had to be better than the terror of uncertainty that these other women must have experienced. They probably did not know what a ponygirl was until they arrived here and saw what she saw today, naked, black hooded women harnessed to wagons and carts. But then again, they were not women. They used to be women, but, like her, their womanhood had been taken away.

Jackie fell asleep quickly and slept soundly. During the night, she awoke when she heard some commotion in the stall next to hers. There was the rattling of chains followed shortly thereafter by the muffled moans of a female voice. It was shortly followed by the grunts from a man's. She realized that the ponygirl next to her was getting raped. The couple went at it like there was no tomorrow and Jackie was sure that she heard the ponygirl come twice before the man grunted and unloaded his spewm into her. Her own pussy burned with lust at the thought that at any time, a man could come by, stretch her bound legs open and insinuate himself into her hot canal. When the couple finished, Jackie went back to sleep.

In the morning, she was startled from sleep when she felt her bindings being undone. A tall, broad shouldered boy, not much over eighteen, hauled her to her feet and made her piss into a strangely shaped port-a-potty. She followed his non-verbal instructions docilely. Her legs were still sore from yesterday's marathon workout. She went through the morning routine quickly. It was pleasant to have her hood off, but disconcerting to have her head shaved again. She ate her food from the ceramic bowl and licked it clean. Her physical efforts of the day before had made her very hungry.

Jackie was somewhat surprised when the young boy pushed her back against the pony stall wall and spread her legs. He raised her knees and began to soap up her intimates. Jackie watched the young man handle her private flesh professionally. He brushed the soap over her nether lips and the skin surrounding her sex and nonchalantly shaved off the small stubble that had grown. When he was done, he paused and looked at her. Jackie wondered how many hairless pussies he had seen in his short adulthood and how many ponygirls he had fucked. Did the cunts look all the same to him, or had he developed an expert's eye for the niceties of intimate female flesh? Naked and defenseless before him, her arms locked securely behind her, she looked at the boy/man through her tiny eyes holes and wondered what he would do next.

Jackie had no experience of the daily routines of a pony barn, routines that hardly varied from estate to estate. She did not know that she would be driven to orgasm every morning of her existence as a ponygirl. The heavyset, baby faced groom smiled at her and then placed his thick hand on her sex. He started to stroke the thin line between her

plump, dark brown labia. Due to the confines of her collar
and the limited range of sight that she had from her hood,
Jackie couldn't see what he was doing, but she sure felt it.
He juices began to flow immediately. He placed his long,
thick thumb in between the softening flesh and drew her
moisture all over her mons. Jackie gave out a low moan.

Satisfied that he had achieved her arousal, the boy drew
the pony's body closer to him by her legs and then ran his
arms under her knees. He was kneeling in front of her, and
he lifted her rear onto his lap. Leaning over, he ran his hot
tongue the length of Jackie's opening slit. She shivered at
the oral caress. He pulled her hips up further and he
grabbed her prominent nub of pleasure between his lips and
began to suck on it gently.

The gag had been restored to Jackie's mouth and her
moan of pleasure reverberated through it. His long, rough
tongue ran the length of her crevasse and then plunged
inside. The ponygirl closed her eyes tightly and reveled in
the oral caresses. The boy seemed an expert at his task.
Roaming his tongue around her labial lips, up to her stiff
clit and back again deeply into her moistened canal, he sent
tantalizing waves of pleasure through the pony's body. Her
shoulders rubbed against the floor as her torso writhed in
response to the oral delight. "Mmmmmmpf! Mmmmmmpf," she yelled out as her lusts rose higher and higher.
Her hips began to shake and her thighs began to quiver.

Sensing that the pony was reaching her point of climax,
the tall, broad shouldered, blond haired groom began to
flick his tongue against Jackie's pulsing pleasure bud. The
excruciating tease to her clit drove Jackie over the top and
she thrust her loins at the taunting mouth. "Ohhhhhhhhh!
Ohhhhhhhh! Ohhhhhhhhhhhhh!" she called out as she
came. Her whole being was concentrated in her pulsing
quim, her body twisted and turned and her legs pumped
furiously in the air. The boy had a firm grip on her thighs

and he relentlessly urged her on with his merciless tongue. "Oooh! Ooooooh! Oooooooooh! Oooooooooooh!" she cried out in a rising crescendo.

Once the ponygirl began to calm, the powerful groom pulled her to her feet by the ring on the end of her gag. He pressed her body up against the rail that ran across her stall and locked her ankles in place. Crawling under the rail, he leashed her collar to a hook in the wall in front of her. He patted the pony affectionately on her rump, took up his equipment, the shaving kit, the feeding bowl, and left the stall.

The ponygirl was breathless as she leaned against the railing. The boy's assault on her loins had come unexpectedly. What a strange world she was in, she thought. Extremes of pleasure and extremes of pain. Reduced to the status of a voiceless, armless animal, and yet groomed with the loving care one might give a child. It was going to be a strange five months.

Normally, Irkut would have been taking the new ponygirl out for her morning training. But today she was scheduled to be marked. He came to her stall and freed her and dragged her behind him on her leash. She tugged and struggled mildly as she was led along, but no more than any other pony new to the bit. The markings were to be applied in the estate tack shop and the tattooist was ready and waiting. After Jackie was carefully and tightly bound in the chair, he meticulously washed and shaved the regions to be tattooed and went right down to work.

The ponygirl began to struggle in the chair as soon as she realized what was going to be done to her. She hadn't forgotten what Jake had said about the tattoos, but she was suddenly revolted at the idea of being marked. It rekindled her fears about whether she was in fact on that guy Burnham's estate. What if she wasn't? Why didn't somebody tell her? She was being marked as someone's property. She didn't want to be anybody's property. She wanted to be Jackie's property and no one else's.

Irkut saw the ponygirl become anxious and unruly in her chair. He had anticipated that. She was bound in extremely tightly and her chest was virtually immobile. However, he didn't want the tattooist distracted and so he landed a hard blow of the thin crop that he had carried with him across the tops of first one and then the other of the pony's thighs.

Jackie's body tensed with the pain and she cried out behind her gag. Her trainer's reaction to her skittishness was quick and resolute. With tears forming in her hidden eyes, she relented her struggles and let the cruel man do his work.

Irkut had thought long and hard about the pony's new name. It was traditional to let their initial trainers name the new ponies. Some favored Greek gods or characters from myths, like Persephone. Some liked daring, action filled names, like Lightning. Irkut had no particular preference as he had named dozens of ponies. He had thought of Ajax, or Paladin, two fierce war-like names to match her somewhat unruly disposition, but he had rejected them. In the end, he was influenced by what everyone was already calling her, 'the chocolate pony'. So he named her 'Chocolate'.

Chocolate gave the most trouble about the ring in her nose. The tattooist, who was also the body jeweler, had vast experience in securing the heads of his charges so that rings could be installed successfully. But in the end, Irkut needed to provide assistance by securing the pony's jaw while the jeweler secured the head.

Chocolate whinnied and cried all the way back to the barn. The golden disks between her thighs jingled as she walked and blood still oozed slightly from her wounds. The angry black dog's head stood out well even on her dark body. Because of her dark brown skin, the tattooist had outlined the heraldic symbol with a thin line of red to set it off. The red eyes and fangs of the dog were clearly visible and, if anything, more ominous since they emerged from the darkness of the dog's head, made even darker by the surrounding flesh.

Jackie was beside herself. Not only was she in excruciating pain from the piercings, but she was appalled that her skin was now permanently marked. And this man, her trainer, he seemed to have an iron will that she could not break. He was coldly efficient in the handling of her. And she feared his whip. She trudged along behind him in her tall, black boots and her matching black hood. He breasts swayed and tremored as she walked. She wondered what name they had given her. She had heard her trainer tell the other man something like, "Shokolodny." The tattooist had laughed. It was, in fact, the Russian word for chocolate.

When they reached the barn, Irkut brought Chocolate in front of a mirror so that she could see her new accouterments. It was standard to show the pony the permanent changes in her body. It helped instill in them the realization that their change in status was also permanent. Ponygirls had to give up on the idea that they were human beings. Thoughts like that only made for misery.

Jackie was shocked at what she saw. She was un-recognizable. The angry dog stared back at her with its demonic red eyes. Her chest was a jumble of two inch high, strange lettering. Her trainer stood next to her, smiling in admiration at her tall, resplendent form. He reached in front of her and massaged her pretty, plump breast. The pony shied back, but he held her in place by grasping her thick nipple between his fingers. With his other hand on her long, black ponytail, he brushed his hand across her thighs and squeezed her nether lips together.

Jackie watched the man take his liberties with her flesh in the mirror. Watching him violate her now marred body at will, something snapped in her. She pushed at the trainer with her hip, causing him to lose his balance and sway back. He released her hair to prevent himself from falling. Jackie turned and kicked out at him with her big black boot, striking him in the thigh. He fell and Jackie scooted past him toward the barn door. She had no idea where she was going. She knew just that she wanted to get away. She had had enough; she wanted out.

Irkut was taken by surprise by the almost unprecedented assault by the ponygirl. He fell to the ground, but was up again in a flash. The barn door was partially closed and it took a second for the armless pony to manage to swing it open using her feet. Just as she was going to take off at full speed, she felt a hand on her ponytail yank her head back sharply. A foot slid under her feet and she flew into the air, landing on her keister. The hand dragged her by her hair to the center of the barn and then let her drop. In an instant, her boots were hooked together.

The pony looked up in anger and fear at her trainer. She knew that she had committed a powerfully wrongful act. But her ire at being manhandled, after all of the depersonalization of her body, was still raging. Irkut grabbed the pony's ankles and lifted them off of the ground. He dragged the pony over to where a long chain dangled from an overhead beam. He clipped the end of the chain to the pony's ankles and then hoisted her up into the air upside down.

Whips were always kept handy in the pony barn and Irkut had no trouble fining one appropriate for his uses. It was a four foot long lash with a thick handle tapering off to a very thin point.

Irkut was angry, but he took a few moments to let his anger cool. Punishment should never be about anger according to his philosophy. It was about teaching a lesson. Beating a pony out of anger was the same as beating a dog or a horse because they acted out. They may need discipline, yes, but within limits and always with a view to their improvement.

Jackie swung back and forth. She was miserably sorry that she had rebelled. She hadn't thought about it, she just did it. And now she was going to pay the price. This was a thousand times worse than having her body molested. It had already been molested at least a dozen times since she arrived and she knew that it would be molested a thousand times more before she was through. This man who ruled her, he would probably abuse her a hundred times before he was finished with her. So what did one caress mean? Nothing. Jackie, fearful and trembling, cursed herself for her stupidity.

The ponygirl whined when she saw her trainer approach her with the whip. She tried vainly to beg for forgiveness, but her words didn't form. Her head was about three feet from the ground and her body was at a perfect angle for the torment of her tender breasts. They felt so exposed, falling 'upwards' toward her chin. Her blood was rushing to her head making her dizzy. She cried when she saw the man pull his strong right hand back for a blow. The whip came towards her as fast as a hornet and the blow that landed across the exposed bottoms of her breasts felt just like a hornet's sting. "Oooooooooom!" the ponygirl cried as she felt the whip's bite. A small crowd of trainers and groom had gathered to watch. A second blow landed across her breasts, just an inch or so closer to the center. The ponygirl's body shook and twisted in response, her piteous moans of pain filling the room, "Ooooooooooooom! Oooooooooooooom!"

Men were holding the leashes of skittish ponygirls as they enjoyed the show. But for the ponygirls, it was something else. It was a vivid reminder of the discipline that they were under and the fact that they could mounted there someday for a real or imagined, or even invented wrong. Or for no reason at all.

Irkut did not stop addressing the ponygirl's ample, firm breasts until he had created a series of red lines across them. He then turned to the front of her thighs. Six strokes he gave her there. She yelled and screamed at each one, begging and pleading for surcease. And then there was the back of her thighs and her plump ass. He belabored the frantically distraught ponygirl mercilessly. She had struck a master. There were few things more serious.

When the determined trainer had finished his assault on her body, the ponygirl was hanging without moving, a long, low moan escaping from the confines over her mouth. Her black ponytail dangled beneath her black clad head. Irkut admired his handiwork. He was a master with a whip and the angry red lines left behind by the whip were all clear and defined. It was just as well that this happened now, he thought. It was early in her training and she would have the benefit of this lesson through the hard days ahead. He knew that it was her sensitivity about being touched and abused that had set the pony off. That and the stress of her new body paintings. But there was no excuse for what she had done. It was time to break her resistance all at once. Therefore, her lesson in comportment must continue.

Last night, the new pony had received the passionate attentions of a number of the trainers and grooms. She had been allowed to reach orgasm several times. He had watched her sweating and groaning in her stall while the men took their pleasure with her. Now, her body would be used without any chance of her own enjoyment.

Irkut removed the gag of the moaning pony. He already had in his hands its replacement and as soon as the thick, leather plug was withdrawn, he shoved it home. It was a thick ring gag.

Jackie felt her mouth jammed open. This was another new experience for her. Her mouth was spread wide and there was a hole in the middle wide enough for the largest, thickest prick. She could feel air rushing into her mouth. She knew what a ring gag was and what it was good for. Her stomach turned as she thought of the abuse she was about to suffer. Her trainer was teaching her a lesson. Anyone could use her, touch her, beat her. She had no right to refuse participation. She would remember it well.

Irkut was the first to avail himself of the liberated, wide open mouth. He stroked his meat a few times to ensure its hardness and then slid it through the leather ring. Jackie coughed and sputtered as it breached her throat. She felt his hand grasp her ponytail and he began, essentially, to jerk off with her head. The pony made slurping sounds as the cock struck home deep inside her throat with each thrust forwards of her head. "Gaaaaa!... Gaaaaa!..... Gaaaaaaa!..." she uttered each time the cock sank home. It was an involuntary noise and it disturbed the ponygirl to make it. It was devastating for her not to have some voluntary part in the use of her body, even if it was merely to spread her legs a little wider or to thrust her hips back at her assailant. But with Irkut's hand on her ponytail and the ring in her mouth, Jackie's wishes and wants regarding this sexual act of assault were of no moment.

The ponygirl trainer luxuriated in the helpless pony's throat. Again and again he penetrated it rudely. Chocolate was choking and gasping for air. He could feel his fluids gathering and after pulling out to allow the pony to gather a deep breath, pushed himself in until he had sunk his whole cock within her. The pony gargled and complained as he held his thick cock in place. It began to pulse and throb in the pony's throat. She could feel the contractions of the long shaft even as she fought for air. His eyes rolled back as the pleasure of his discharge rolled through him. Finally, when he was done, he withdrew his still hard prick.

Chocolate gasped for breath when her airway was finally freed. She hoped and prayed that her punishment was at an end. The man had made a dramatic demonstration of his power over her and the consequences of disobedience. She vowed to obey him in all things.

But the ponygirl's punishment was not over. Irkut walked over to one of the many equipment closets and withdrew two penis-like, steel items from it. He returned to the pony girl and placed the shorter and fatter one in his pocket while he made an adjustment to the longer, thinner one. He asked one of the other trainers for assistance. The other man took Jackie's knees and pulled them apart so that her pudendum was exposed. Irkut began to tickle and caress it until it began to lubricate. He then took the steel dildo and, covering its tip with the pony's moisture slid it into her crevasse. He then went to her back and, after drooling a large gob of spit onto the shorter, fatter device, plunged it into the small entrance in the pony's rear. Chocolate moaned as the tissues of her rectum were torn to accommodate the large presence. Irkut made an adjustment to the base of the object before he plunged it fully in.

He then stepped back and waited.

Jackie whined with self pity as she felt her private places invaded. She could only conceive of a nefarious purpose in filling her thusly, although she could not conceive what it could be. Her knees had been released and her thighs squeezed her pussy tightly around the long, cold dildo lodged there. At first, there was just a tingle. Then there was a small shock that made her jump. That was followed by a long, intense electrical charge flowing through the walls of her canal. Her innards cringed as the jolt of battery powered electricity caused her womb to cramp. She howled at the pain. Just as the charge dwindled and she was able to regain her breath, a similar, painful charge erupted in her bowels. Her body twisted and turned as she tried to fight off the excruciating effects of the shock. She whined and cried and begged for mercy, sounds that emerged from her distended lips only as a series of unintelligible ejaculations.

The dildos were specially designed with powerful batteries set to deliver random, intense, charges of electricity to the pony's innards over a period of thirty minutes. In the meantime, her mouth was still available and the trainers and grooms lined up to take advantage of it. When the charges went off, Chocolate delivered an intense vibrato of expressed pain to the pricks that invaded her mouth and throat, enlivening, for her assailants, the experience of occupying it. Each time it went off with a prick buried deeply within her, her throat constricted around the stiff tube of meat, delivering great delight to the prick's owner while her body shook and shivered from the pain.

To Jackie, the half hour seemed like forever. She had never known pain like this, pain that pierced her whole body. Just when she felt that she could not survive another jolt, one would come, in her pussy or her ass, or both at once, and she would howl with anguish.

While the fierce charges of electricity ran through her, something amazing from such small devices, Jackie was wholly unconscious of the stiff pricks that invaded her mouth and throat, but as soon as the jolt subsided, she would experience the callous presence in her mouth darting back and forth, forcing itself down her throat or reveling in the heat of her mouth. Each time one of the men unloaded their sticky white discharge into her mouth or throat, another would prepare to take his place and the pony would whine and moan in self pity.

It was a miserable, broken pony that was later lowered from her chain. She was dragged to her stall and mounted against her rail. Her nose ring was still too sensitive to be used to affix her to the wall and so it was the ring in her gag, which had been replaced, that was connected to the chain.

Jackie cried and cried as she remained forcibly standing, alone in her stall. She had discovered a new level of misery and pain. She had thought that she could preserve a part of her self, some small kindling of her independence and will that would burst back into fullness when she had done her time as a ponygirl. But she could see now that that would not be possible. These men intended to crush her, to make her become in her mind what they had made of her exterior, a lowly beast subject to their whims. "Oh, God," she cried to her deity as her body recalled its recent abuse, "help me bear this, help me survive!"

CHAPTER ELEVEN
RECONCILIATION

Over the next few days, Lightning returned to her normal routine. Grobgy had left orders for her special treatment and all of the trainers and grooms were especially kind to her. On the second day, she was taken out for a light workout. She returned from it, energized and refreshed. When she entered the barn, she was diverted from her normal route to one of the stalls and brought into the common area. She felt nervous when she saw the several men gathered there. They called out to her when they saw her. What could this be, the ponygirl wondered. What were they planning for her?

When she was brought within the circle of men, Lightning saw what all the excitement was about. Kneeling there, on top of a thick, plaited rug, was her lover, Persephone. Her gag had been removed and she was kneeling with her back straight up, her thighs spread. Lightning felt her bit being removed and she was led to kneel down in front of her lover.

Lightning had performed for the men many times before. Usually, it was some pony who she knew by sight alone. She had had intimate contact, in the sense of contact that was prolonged and during which she was able to get to know some aspect of her personality, with only one pony, the blond tailed pony which was kneeling in front of her right now. Her heart leapt as she saw the other pony's plump breasts and the familiar writing across her chest. Persephone perked up too as she recognized Lightning in return.

Lightning was unaware of the fact that her affinity for the other pony was well known. They had purposely been kept apart, except for their recent escapades in the summer pasture. Emotional connections between ponygirls were not encouraged. But Grobgy had ordered it as part of Lightning's rehabilitation.

Many times while in the pasture, Lightning and Persephone had been able to brush their fevered lips together and give each other pleasure. But they had been wearing their bits and were unable to deeply penetrate each other's orifices. But here they were; their mouths were freed. And the circle of lustful men were more than encouraging them to unite in passion, they were ordering them to.

Lightning leaned forward and pressed her plump lips upon the other pony's. She was met with a pliant, encouraging response. She parted her lips and let her tongue dance across the inner portion of Persephone's lips. As she did so, she heard the other pony sigh. Her tongue was met by the other's and Lightning relished the heat that flowed between them. She pressed her lips up hard against her lover's and their bodies met. Lightning could feel the heat of the other pony's body from her breasts down to her hips and her thighs. The only thing missing from their lustful embrace was their arms, pulling each other in tightly. But Lightning hardly missed them. She was in heaven.

The men were drawn into a circle around the loving ponies and gave them vocal encouragement. Lightning felt Persephone's mouth disengage from hers. The pony dipped her head and seized one of Lightning's breasts with her lips. She sucked on the nipple at first tenderly, circling her tongue across the areola. But then her passion took control of her and she began to suck on it hungrily, drawing it deep into her mouth, capturing it with her teeth.

Lightning groaned at the sudden escalation of her lover's passion. She let her body fall to its side and the other pony followed suit. Her mouth found Persephone's breast and she returned the passionate caress.

Lightning was aware of the lustful eyes that were taking in her Sapphic display. But she did not care. It had many weeks since she had had full access to her lover's body and she certainly had no qualms about making a display of passion before the masters, who had all seen her in the throes of orgasm many times. Turning head to foot, Lightning kissed her lover's tummy, lapped at her lower belly and then laid her long, sensuous, well trained tongue across her nether lips. There was a brief struggle between the ponies as to who would lay on top, but Persephone soon gave in to the taller, stronger pony. They made the two backed beast before the men, supping at each other's loins, lapping up each other's precious discharge. Lightning felt the other pony's body stiffen and then begin to jerk and she knew that she had brought her to completion. Her tongue was buried deep in her quim and she could feel the contractions of the pussy's walls.

The aroma of her lover's oozing lust almost made her swoon. She could feel the other's loving tongue on and in her canal and the heat of her loins was spreading over her entire body. Her orgasm struck her like a bolt of electricity and her body tightened and her thighs clamped around the blue clad head between them. Wave after wave of pleasure flowed through her as the tongue of her former cart mate continued its caresses to her loins. Her own shrouded head was still buried between her lover's thighs and she felt her rise to her second crisis, her hips bucking wildly, her voice moaning her ecstasy.

It was after Lightning's third orgasm that she felt a gentle tug on her long, rust colored ponytail. Reluctantly, she raised her head from between her lover's thighs and rose from her body. It was the men's turn to assuage their lusts and the ponygirls were now required to remedy the passions they had raised in their audience. Lightning gratefully accepted the cock of one of the trainers in her mouth. He was sitting on a bench, his thighs spread wide and his cock peaking out of his pants. Lightning ran her tongue around the bulbous head and then dragged her tender lips down its length. She soon had the trainer groaning with pleasure and she reaped the reward of his hot spunk.

Two of the men had the ponies kneel back down on the rug, bent over face to face, so that their lips just touched. The men knelt behind them and pierced their already moist and loose canals with their stiffened pricks. Lightning moaned as the man possessed her and her lips sought her lover's. The ponies groaned and panted with pleasure as their pussies were plowed by the men. Lightning rocked her hips back and forth as she sought maximum contact with the long, thick cock inside her. Her tongue danced in Persephone's mouth. When she felt the man's cock begin to pulse and throb within her, splashing his cum into her womb, she came again. She thrust her face hard up against Persephone's and mashed her lips firmly against hers. If she could have, she would have thrust her whole body down her lover's throat and so became one with her.

When the men were through with them, Lightning and Persephone were taken to their stalls. Later that afternoon, when their training runs were completed, they lay entwined with each other in the shade of the tall oak tree in the summer pasture. It was a tender, wonderful few hours that they spent. That day was the high point of Lightning's life as a ponygirl, although she could not have known it then. In early August, when training began in earnest for the fall season, Persephone was sold off to another estate which was looking for a good runner for a four pony, brougham team.

But for now, all was well. The ponies continued to spend their free time together in the pony pasture, including in their attentions the tall, Australian pony and one or two others who sought physical solace with them. Lightning learned a trick from watching the other ponies. If one pony leaned its front against the back of a sitting pony, wrapping her thighs around her hips, the sitting pony could use her bound and otherwise useless hands to fondle and caress the kneeling pony's pussy. She moaned and groaned with delight when she felt Persephone's hands rub against her inner thighs and stroke her sex. When she came, her breasts crushed against Persephone's back, her shrouded head leaning over her shoulder, her whole body shook with pleasure.

Drabik, in spite of Grobgy's orders, stayed away from the pony for two weeks. He was training a new pony, a strong, sturdy, former Polish female. She had thick legs and arms and a broad back. He had his doubts about her, since she had little speed. But it was something to do to wile the summer away.

And he spent at least two afternoons a week with Anya. She had become an earnest and capable cock sucker and had come to appreciate the pleasurable aspects of the use of her narrow, rear passage.

It was the second week in July when Drabik decided he had postponed the inevitable for too long. It was ironic to him that he was being ordered to resume the 'relationship' if you could call it that, between himself and the auburn tailed pony when he had been trying to destroy it. But he had thought it out carefully. He was over her. Whatever magic she had worked on him had been dispelled by her brutal beating. It had taken a few days, but the destruction of his emotional bond to the pony was complete. He could and would use her just like any other pony.

It was in the early evening that he came to her. Lightning was mounted in her stall, having eaten her bland dinner. She had spent a wonderful afternoon with her lover in the pony pasture and her fragrance lingered in her mind. She didn't know how long her summer vacation would last. She knew that her career as a racing ponygirl was not at an end, but she would enjoy the lassitude of the current pace of living as long as it lasted.

She heard the stall door open and shut behind her and she closed her eyes in readiness for physical contact. It was the time that the trainers, their assistants or some of the more favored staff would come and avail themselves of the exposed orifices of the ponygirls. Lightning didn't mind. It helped pass the time and some of the men were quite considerate lovers, deriving their sexual satisfaction both from their own explosive climaxes, but also from the thrill of watching and feeling the throes of passion of a ponygirl.

Lightning saw rough hands unclasp her nose ring from the chain that led to the wall and felt her waist and ankles freed. Strong arms twisted her body around. Sometimes this was done when the man wanted her to suckle him to completion or to fuck her on the floor, either bent over on her knees, or face to face. But when she turned to look at the face of her prospective lover, she was appalled and shocked to see who it really was. Her body began to shake and her knees got weak. "Not him! Not him!" she cried to herself. Tears formed in her eyes.

Why was he so cruel to her? Why did he hate her? There was a time when she had felt that he had loved her and when she was ready to love him too. In fact, she had adored him, made him into her god. She would do anything for him. But he had rejected her cruelly and now was only a source of fear to her.

She felt his hands on her shoulders as he pressed her to her knees. He unbuckled her gag and removed it, freeing her mouth. He looked down at the blue headed ponygirl. She was no different from the others. She wasn't human. He couldn't love a beast. She existed to be used as a thing of pleasure and to serve her masters by obedience and travail. The callous trainer removed his stiffening prick from his pants and presented it to the ponygirl. He didn't speak to her. He had nothing to say, and even if he did, one didn't talk to ponygirls. It would be like talking to a dog.

He felt the pretty lips of the pony engulf him and he sighed as he felt the transferred heat on his cock. He had his hand firmly on her tail and guided the blue clad head back and forth over his tool.

Lightning accepted the hard meat of her tormentor without resistance. She felt her head being moved up and down on the cruel man's rigid cock and accommodated the rhythm by pursing her lips around its shaft and dutifully washing the prick's head with her tongue.

But then something broke inside her. She had tried to forget her torture at this man's hands. She had tried to forget her unhappiness and dismay of his abandonment of her. But all of those feelings rushed into her mind at once. She began to sob. At first quietly and without breaking her stride, but then, despite her efforts to quell it, her grief just overcame her and her jaw slackened and her lips forgot their task. She sobbed and sobbed unlike she had ever done before, worse than when she had first found herself so cruelly bound, gagged and hooded as a ponygirl.

Drabik was taken aback by the pony's reaction. At one second she was obediently servicing his conscienceless prick and the next she was bawling uncontrollably, his cock lying fallow in her mouth.

The dreaded assassin and pony trainer was astounded. Certainly he expected her to be afraid. But that was the point, wasn't it? They were all supposed to be afraid of him. Everyone. Even Anya and her asshole father, Grobgy. He pushed her head back from his cock and saw the trembling lips of the overcome pony. Suddenly, all of the emotions that he had been fighting, that he had thought dead, came rushing to the fore. He knelt and took the ponygirl in his arms, clutching her to his body. She rested her head on his shoulder and sobbed. He felt her naked breasts pressed against him as her chest heaved with each mournful wail.

Drabik was at a loss what to do. He grabbed the pony by the head and began to stroke it, rubbing it. His passion for this pony was rising. Her grief touched him as her pain had not. He placed his lips on hers and kissed her.

Lightning felt her trainer's lips upon hers. Their heat burned her. When his tongue entered her mouth, her sobs turned to moans. It was what she wanted, yearned for. She wanted forgiveness for whatever it was that she had done, forgiveness for her very existence. She pressed her body closely against the man's, her breasts mashed into his chest. She wanted him, wanted him to enter her. With all of her silent earnestness she begged him, with her lips, her tongue and her body.

Drabik felt himself being drawn inexorably into union with the ponygirl. He pushed her back and pulled his cotton shirt over his head, baring his hairy black chest. He untied his boots and removed his pants.

Now he knelt up against the pony as naked as she. Their skin drew sparks where it connected and Drabik pushed the pony down onto its back. She spread her legs expectantly, joyfully. Every part of her yearned for his cock, needed him to possess her. When she felt the head of his stiff prick probe at her opening, she sighed with delight.

As his piece slid home into her soft, wet channel, she moaned.

Drabik's mind clouded over as he felt himself sink deeply into the ponygirl's recesses. The tight, wet warmth of her cunt delighted him. He lay atop her, his belly pressed into hers, his hands on her shoulders and he found her mouth again. He was proud of his ability to control his lust, at the slow, determined way that he took his pleasures. But now he was in rut. His hips slammed against the pony's as he pumped his cock in and out of her pussy with rapid intensity. The ponygirl moaned her passion into his mouth as her lusts were driven higher and higher.

To Lightning, this was the culmination of all of her dreams. She wanted love, wanted to be special. She wanted the lust of the man who had broken her, taught her her new life and who was the world to her. She wanted his spunk inside her and drove back against his hips with each thrust. Her legs were splayed wide as her pussy accepted each plunging thrust with joy. She felt her moment of crisis approaching. She took her long, strong, ponygirl legs and wrapped them around her trainer's. With her ankles and feet, she tried to draw him into her deeper and deeper.

Drabik felt his fluids massing in his balls, raging for release. He was waiting, waiting, waiting for the pony's climax to begin. But he could not hold out any longer. He felt his cum flow down his cock and pour into the ponygirl's accepting and welcoming womb. He groaned with each pulse of his cock, his body stiffening, his hands gripping the head of the ponygirl tightly, his tongue dancing madly with hers.

Lightning felt her master come and her own floodgates released. Hard, repetitive, rhythmic contractions exploded in her womb. She felt the man's hot seed inside her and her mind was overwhelmed with joy. She shouted her passion into her master's mouth, "Ahhhhhhhhhhh!

Ahhhhhhhhhhhh!" as he groaned back. It was a new language they had discovered together, one which they intuitively understood. Their souls were matched, their bodies chemically reactive.

As they lay, exhausted by their passions, each of them knew that some line had been crossed. Either the cruel, hard trainer would love her or he would have to destroy her. There was no other way.

End of Book Four